Here Comes
Mrs. Kugelman

Here Comes Mrs. Kugelman

—◄◦►—

A NOVEL

MINKA PRADELSKI

Translated from the German by

Philip Boehm

METROPOLITAN BOOKS

HENRY HOLT AND COMPANY

NEW YORK

Metropolitan Books
Henry Holt and Company, LLC
Publishers since 1866
175 Fifth Avenue
New York, New York 10010
www.henryholt.com

Metropolitan Books® and m® are registered trademarks of
Henry Holt and Company, LLC.

Originally published in Germany in 2005 under the title *Und da kam Frau Kugelmann*
by Frankfurter Verlagsanstalt

Distributed in Canada by Raincoast Book Distribution Limited

Library of Congress Cataloging-in-Publication Data

Pradelski, Minka.
  [Und da kam Frau Kugelmann. English]
Here comes Mrs. Kugelman : a novel / Minka Pradelski. — First edition.
    pages   cm
ISBN 978-0-8050-8212-8
I. Title.
PT2676.R265U5313 2013
833'.92—dc23

2012046243

Henry Holt books are available for special promotions and premiums.
For details contact: Director, Special Markets.

First Edition 2013

Designed by Meryl Sussman Levavi

Printed in the United States of America

1 3 5 7 9 10 8 6 4 2

For Arno Lustiger, Siegmund Pluznik,

and all Będziners

Contents

—◀◦▶—

Here Comes
Mrs. Kugelman

1

The silver chest

I DIDN'T LEARN OF MY AUNT HALINA'S DEATH UNTIL A whole month after she had passed away or, more precisely, three hours after the lawyer serving as her executor read out her will. My relatives know that my unusual eating habits make it difficult for me to travel and I can't just go flying off to Tel Aviv on the spur of the moment. So when she died, it never occurred to them to let me know.

The lawyer sent an itemized list of what she'd left me: one small brown suitcase, approximately seventy years old, and one silver chest lined with red velvet containing eight forks and nine knives of a fish service that once had twelve settings.

Halina's children had no idea why she had included me at all, and I couldn't figure out the reason for the old suitcase and the incomplete fish service, given that I hardly ever travel anywhere and never touch fish. I've refused to eat fish since I was little, to distance myself from my mother, a notorious murderess of fish. Every Friday morning, our bathtub was home to a young carp darting back and forth in the water until it wound up on a cutting board where my mother chopped it into pieces. And every week I watched with a fresh shudder of nausea as the cut-up bits twitched for an hour as if still alive. In my bed at night, I willed the quivering fragments to grow back together and the fish to jump off the board and splash into the tub and swim out the window into the river, where the muddy green current would carry it out to sea. Then it could swim back to our house the next Friday.

Of course I could have had the suitcase and the fish service shipped to me. But I wanted to collect my inheritance in person. And the suitcase might just bring me luck, I thought, since I'm desperately searching for a husband. Maybe I'll find one in Tel Aviv. Several months ago I was struck by an intense desire to get married: out of the blue I started yearning for dishes spilling out of the sink and stacks of clothes to iron, and nothing seemed more appealing than the deafening screams of little babies. By chance I discovered a playground near my apartment, where I loved to watch the children ride the seesaw and totter around. I peered curiously into every passing stroller and was quickly able to tell a child's precise age down to the day. Soon after that I mastered baby talk. Infants would reach for me with their tiny arms; toddlers started to crawl in my direction or stagger over on their shaky little legs, just to be near me. But I didn't give much thought to this development until my neighbor's one-year-old pronounced her first word, my name, and gazed at me, full of expectation, to the horror of her parents, whose relationship with me is strained because of the nighttime noise coming from my apartment. Luckily I recognized this was a signal from my own children—a sign of their wish to be born. And now I've made up my mind: I, Tsippy Silberberg, am going to start a family.

Halina's bequest is a further sign. Maybe I'll meet an attractive man on the beach and ask him whether he likes fish, even though I'll never eat it under any circumstances. If he knows how to handle a fish service and can spin a good story about the fate of the missing forks, I'll marry him on the spot.

I ARRIVE AT the beach hotel in Tel Aviv late in the afternoon, after a trying flight, with sweaty clothes and swollen feet. When I ask for my room, I learn that someone else has already claimed it and is using *my* bathroom, tracking sand onto *my* floor, and sleeping in the bed *I* had booked.

"That room has just been taken," says the clerk, softening his voice to convey his regrets. Apparently a young woman had shown up two hours earlier and asked for the room being held for Silberberg. And now the clerk's telling me that he's very sorry but he doesn't have any other room for me for the next several days.

What am I supposed to do, make a scene in front of the whole hotel? Summon all the guests to the lobby and proclaim that I am the real Silberberg, the Silberberg who reserved a room for ten days in the middle of August, the hottest month of the year, when the thick, wet heat coats your body with a sticky haze, and you sweat and sweat and can barely breathe? Do I have to explain to the clerk that I'm the Silberberg who deserves their best sea-view room? Because before I left Germany I resolved to break free from my cold green passion, and this room is my reward.

This passion is really an addiction—a frozen food addiction, in fact, that propels me to the kitchen at three in the morning, after a short, dreamless sleep. I open the freezer and rip the vegetables out of their bags; I crush the icy clusters with my naked hands, scrape the frosty crust off beans, snap bits of corn and broccoli from off their crystal chains, gently massage the precooked vegetable wedges until they come apart, then stuff the frigid morsels into my mouth. I have known nights of unbridled gluttony when no frozen package escaped my craving. When I would rip each one open and devour the icy delicacies but find no peace. When, still despairing, I would return the empty package to the freezer so I could then hold it against my flushed cheeks to soothe the burning. And there I would sit, until the pale light of morning had calmed me enough that I could go back to bed, with bloated belly and trembling hands.

To completely surrender to my icy passion would mean living at the supermarket in a walk-in freezer, surrounded by open cartons, my head resting on an ice pack, an ice-crowned queen in a wonderland of frozen bounty.

*   *   *

"I DEMAND TO see this woman, with her ID and proof of her reservation!" I snap at the clerk—if he thinks I'm going to settle for an apology he's got another thought coming.

"Please, Miss. This is a hotel, not a police station."

All right, so the sharp voice didn't work. Maybe if I scream loud enough the other Silberberg will come out of my room and introduce herself with the name I've had since birth. Then we'll see whether I am who I say I am and can keep on being Tsippy Silberberg, or whether this upstart has taken possession of me completely. Within seconds all hell will break loose and the guests will split into three factions: those who side with the clerk, those in favor of the fake Silberberg, and those who support me. They'll whip one another into a fury: first they'll start calling each other names and soon they'll be bludgeoning each other with beach bags and newspapers and cameras. The lobby will run with blood, doctors will race to the battlefield to tend the wounded before dispatching them to nearby hospitals.

"I booked a room and I'm going to have it," I say.

The clerk sees I'm on the verge of shouting.

"Please, Miss. We'll find you a better room for half the price, in a four-star hotel." He turns away, dials a number, and hands me a calling card with the name and address of a nearby establishment.

"Here you go," he says in an encouraging, fatherly tone, "I'm sure you'll find it very much to your liking." The bell-hop is already carrying out my suitcase, and I chase after him with my hand luggage.

* * *

HMMM. CAN THERE really be another Silberberg from some other German city with a reservation for the same dates who's now relaxing in my room? Or is this woman in fact a Silberstein who bribed the clerk to find her a room and wound up with mine since our names are so similar? If my name were Goldberg, I could have checked in long ago, but then I never would have met Mrs. Kugelman.

FROM THE MOMENT I laid eyes on her I knew that this woman had to have a round-sounding name like Kegel or Kugel—"bowling ball" or "cannonball"—because everything about her is round: eyes and ears, head, hips, legs, stomach. She looks as if she were constructed of a stack of spheres—a small one for the head, a large one for the body, and four stretched into ovals for arms and legs. Only the wrinkles in her face defy the roundness and go digging into her skin wherever they want. And her shoes have a different shape as well: large foot beds with little laces: orthopedic sandals from a German shoe factory—elderly ladies in Israel swear by orthopedic shoes made in Germany.

And I was right, too: her name really is Kugelman; she brought it all the way from Poland and has no intention of letting it go, particularly since she's almost lost it twice— the first time when it vanished behind a number; and then, after it was restored, when she came to Israel. Her new country wanted to take the beautiful name that was so perfectly matched to her appearance, and replace it with a new Hebrew name. And with that, she could begin a completely new life, just as though she'd been touched by a wand.

Knowing Mrs. Kugelman, I'm sure she refused to give up her name. I can easily see her writing directly to the prime minister: Esteemed Mr. Ben-Gurion, even though you are the first prime minister of Israel and even though you have a lovely new name, I prefer to keep my old one, since it suits me so well. Maybe she sent along a picture of herself to convince the prime minister. And maybe the prime minister was convinced enough to suggest that the immigration office give her not a completely new name but just a translated one—turning "Kugel" into a ball in Hebrew and replacing the "Man" with "Ben," or "son." So Kugelman would become been Ben Kadur, or son of a ball, a name similar to Ben-Gurion, or son of Gurion, and Mrs. Kugelman would surely be happy with a name like that, a good name for a good new life in Israel.

Undoubtedly Mrs. Kugelman thought long and hard before responding to the authorities and thanking Ben-Gurion for the suggestion, but why should she take a name she didn't like? Even if the son of Gurion had proposed calling her daughter of a ball, which he hadn't, it wouldn't have changed anything: she simply didn't want the new name. And besides, how could a new name, especially one like that, make her into a new person? Couldn't she become a new person with her old name, just by forgetting everything that had happened? Or else go on being who she was and not forget anything, including the fact that once upon a time she'd lived in Poland, in the town of Będzin.

AND THAT'S THE Mrs. Kugelman who barges into my room very early in the morning on my first day in Tel Aviv: a woman who kept her name and didn't forget a thing—especially about the town of Będzin.

"The management sent me," she explains, "to see if everything's in order." She pretends to inspect the bathroom, checking for soap and toilet paper, and tests for dust on the shelves or ash in the ashtray, but then out of the blue she pulls up a chair right next to my bed.

"You're all alone here, aren't you?" she asks gently.

"What makes you think that?"

"Yesterday when you arrived in the lobby I was watching you. I can always tell when a girl is on her own. By the way she moves. Single women don't look around. They don't want anybody to notice that no one is waiting for them."

"Would you please leave?" I say, annoyed.

"Most guests ask me to stay."

"Well, I'm not most guests. Leave this minute or I'll call the front desk."

She leaves. Half an hour later there is a knock at the door.

"I thought I'd stop by again. Do you have time for me now?" she asks when I open the door a crack, and pushes right past me into my sparsely furnished room.

I have to get rid of this woman, I say to myself, and ask her to leave.

The next thing I know she's out in the hallway, clumsily shoving a chair up to my closed door, and there she sits. I peek through the peephole: incredible—she's sitting there without moving a muscle, patiently waiting.

"How long are you planning to stay there?" I call out.

"As long as it takes for you to let me in," she answers casually.

"What is it that you want?"

"To talk to you."

She obviously has no intention of leaving me in peace. The next thing I know the whole floor will start complaining and blame me for the noise; they'll say I have no compassion for the elderly, they'll call me heartless for leaving a woman who could very well be my mother sitting in the hall like that. So I fling open the door and ask her in.

"You don't work for the hotel. Who are you?"

"I'm as much part of this hotel as the sofas and chairs."

"What's that supposed to mean?"

"I come here every day and wait."

"For what, the messiah?"

"But now the waiting's over, at least for the next few days."

"You mean he's finally come?"

"If you want, I'll stay with you and help you pass the time."

"What if I don't want?"

"I'll tell you stories from my school days."

"I won't listen."

"Listen to just one little story from Będzin."

"I'm not interested in Benzene."

"That's not how you say it. Try it softer, with more feeling. The letters need to run together like chocolate melting on your tongue. Here, have some."

And she actually hands me a piece of chocolate. I sniff it and pop it in my mouth. The name isn't so hard to say, I think. Who could imagine that popping chocolate into your mouth was a good way to learn Polish pronunciation. Maybe if I were addicted to sweets or chocolate bars or cream cakes or ice cream or caramels, then I'd be able to say all sorts of words in Polish and possibly even pick up a few other Slavic languages.

"Where is this Będzin?" I ask hesitantly.

"Not far from Katowice," she answers.

Katowice, in Upper Silesia. Right near my father's hometown.

OF COURSE STORIES from her school days are the last thing I want to hear about. I hated school. If she starts talking about school I'm going to grab my bikini, dash out of the room, run down to the beach, and stretch out right next to the fake Silberberg, or better yet, take her place. Even if Mrs. Kugelman begs me or ties me to the bed and gags me, I don't want to hear about any school.

Except how am I supposed to tell an old lady, probably a survivor, that I don't want to hear her story? She leans in and grabs on to me, whispering urgently in my ear:

"Listen carefully to what I have to say. Don't run away. I have to talk to you or else my town will die."

"Well, I might die if you start talking about school."

"Just hear me out a little. You won't believe what I have to tell you about my school. All our teachers and all the students are alive. Right here in Israel."

"You mean that some of them survived?"

"No. I'm just saying that they're alive, every last one of them."

"Every last one of them survived in a small town in Poland? I don't believe it."

"Not the way you think. There's a group of us classmates who keep them alive. We tell stories about them. We dust off the years, rub in the polish, and work and knead and massage everything until it's supple and smooth, and before you know it they're up and moving."

"You mean they literally move?"

"Most people can't see them. But you're one of those who can."

"Me?"

"Yes, you."

"How do I know what you're telling me is true?"

"Oh, there's no end of truths in Będzin. There's a whole mountain of truths inside every single thing that happens. One day there were one hundred twenty thousand truths in Będzin. See, now you're getting curious."

"Yes," I said, turning red, and somehow feel caught out.

"Just keep listening and I'll tell you how it was. When you looked down the main street, which ran through the middle of town, the first thing you saw was the church, which was much taller than the synagogue on account of the steeple, and was probably much older as well. But the synagogue was right in front of the church: a great big flat gray building you couldn't miss. So it's a good guess that the Jews saw only the synagogue, the Christians saw only the church, and the nonbelievers saw nothing except the boundless horizon, and that means there were already about as many truths in Będzin as there were people—let's say forty thousand. But I remember a day when all in the blink of an eye, these truths multiplied to three times as many, when each person looked from the church to the synagogue to the sky and each person saw all three. That means a hundred and twenty thousand truths. That day had started just like any other but turned into a nightmare when the Christians went mad and fixed their eyes on the damned synagogue and set upon it and the Jews stared at the damned church that was the source of their suffering. Even the atheists stopped gazing at the boundless horizon and noticed the world of the here and now and the damned houses of God where the masses were being drugged with the opium of religion. So how many truths were there in Będzin on that day? It's impossible to count."

Mrs. Kugelman stares at me. I'm at a loss for words. Taking advantage of my silence, she quickly introduces herself.

"My name is Bella, by the way," she says, with a broad, winning smile. "Everyone at school knew who I was because of my blond braids. They were so thick and long that most of my schoolmates tried pulling them at one time or another just to see if they were real. They never pulled a second time, though; I made sure of that. One chance to check and that was that." She shot me a brief glance, sensed my interest, and went on.

"Out of my whole high school class only four went through the terrible times and came out alive: handsome Adam, the proud Polish girl, myself, and my cousin Golda who stayed in Poland.

"When Adam and the Polish girl were still in good health, we used to meet regularly here in Tel Aviv, in Adam's apartment. As soon as he let me in the door he'd ask if he could pull my braids, even though my hair's been short and gray for years. Usually the Polish girl was there, too, and the two would grab at the air where my braids used to be their thickest. If they pulled too hard I'd cry out in pain, but they seldom did that.

"Every time we sat down on Adam's sofa to talk, the strangest thing happened: the door to the apartment seemed to open and close by itself, and all sorts of familiar figures started filling up the room.

"Then, just like that, we'd hear cobblers hammering away, we'd see tailors snipping at their fabric, we'd taste the delicious food sold on the street, and we'd hear the lively mix of Polish and Yiddish we knew so well—all the sounds of the butchers and bakers, the merchants and the manufacturers, the porters and the beggars. If one of us coughed, we would race in our minds to Gabłoński's drugstore for some of his bitter cough syrup, then hurry around the corner, past Lachman's barbershop, to get something sweet next door at Potok's. Sometimes the room was full to bursting, with girls in dark blue blouses and red hat-ribbons squeezing into the corners and boys with ice skates or wet swimsuits crowding through the door. Marysia Teitelbaum's little poodle Kajtuś would run around in circles, so excited he didn't know who to greet first. Pani Kleinowa, our nervous Polish teacher, was the first of the staff to turn up, followed by Fanny Sternenlicht, our beautiful Latin teacher, wearing those fetching ankle boots of hers—she really loved to fluster her students. Then our math teacher, Professor Rado—his face was nothing to look at, let me tell you—marched into the room with small but determined steps, followed by our skinny Christian caretaker Kowalski with his son Bolek. And after them came all the school groups and political clubs, the Zionists and Bundists and whoever else, until everyone who'd disappeared was right there with us once again.

"On and on it went, street after street, house after house, until our Będzin rose up before our eyes, just the way it had been—a hardworking little Jewish town in Polish Silesia, just within sight of the German border, smack in the middle of the busy coal district called Zagłębie—such a musical name don't you think?"

"WE ALL LIVED on Małachowski Street," Mrs. Kugelman hurries on—"me, the proud Polish girl, and sly Gonna, just a few houses apart from each other. Moniek lived in an imposing house right next to the Fürstenberg mansion, which belonged to the man who'd donated the money to start our school. Mietek, the poor devil, lived much farther down, in one of the dilapidated rear houses that were hidden behind the magnificent buildings that lined the street—a stranger wouldn't even know they existed. Handsome Adam lived farther out, with the Poles, by his father's soap factory. Oh, I almost forgot: my best friend, Kotek, also lived on Małachowski Street, a little higher up than us, on the square named after the third of May, the day when Poland first proclaimed its constitution.

"We actually had two main avenues, real boulevards, Małachowski Street, which was very grand, and Kołłątaj Street, which was very elegant. Both were broad enough for whole regiments to march up and down on holidays. From Kołłątaj Street you could look between the buildings and catch glimpses of the synagogue. It was in the neighborhood where the very pious Jews lived, a little uphill from the market, which was always bustling with peddlers from the nearby villages who never stopped hawking their wares. At the market, each voice was louder than the next, but by the time they drifted down the streets to us they sounded smaller, like children at a playground. Higher up on the hill you could see King Casimir's ancient castle, with its enormous, stately park. And on the other side was our old modest cemetery, built on terraces cut into the hill and shaded by magnificent trees, with Hebrew inscriptions on the gravestones, all facing east, toward Jerusalem. Just next to it, separated by a narrow path, was the Christian cemetery, with crosses and flowers, neatly arranged in tight rows. And a little ways past the cemeteries was the poor district, where if it was quiet you could hear our river, the Black Przemsza, gently hugging the bank, splashing along peacefully, pleased to carry the dark waters from the coal mines in Dąbrowa, the neighboring town, to us in Będzin."

2

A magic coat and a man with a dream

MRS. KUGELMAN COUGHS BUT TRIES TO KEEP TALKING anyway, as if she fears that a break might end my willingness to listen, and then she'll have to fight for my attention all over again.

"IN THE MORNINGS," she goes on, "while we were in school, the boulevards belonged to the grown-ups. Silesians came in from across the border to shop for cheap goods, and farmers from all around came to Będzin to buy things as well. One of the shopkeepers on Kołłątaj Street, Jacob Teitelbaum, used to take advantage of the gullible peasants. He was the best and fastest salesman in town, though you'd never guess it from the way he looked. He kept his wavy, bright red hair cut short and combed back, and you hardly even noticed him as he stood among the racks of clothes, humbly waiting for the next customer.

"Teitelbaum used to pay a few pennies to a couple of

his relatives, Samek and Poldek, to shill for him in the street—two young brothers with curly, ginger-colored hair. They would shout and wave their hands to stop passersby, and then coax them into Teitelbaum's shop with flattering words. Every person who followed the brothers into the store wound up buying a coat. And when they left the store, they'd run away as fast as the wind. And they'd always be wearing their thick new fluffy winter coats—even on the hottest days of the year. You know why?"

I found myself shaking my head.

She glanced at me and went on: "It was like this. Teitelbaum always kept a bundle of bills close at hand. Whenever someone from the country—never the town, mind you—asked for a coat, he would secretly stuff a couple of bills into a pocket, quick as lightning. Then he helped the customer into the prepared coat. The minute the farmer stuck his hand inside the pocket, he would find the bills smiling at him through the thickly woven cloth, and that was that, the spell was cast. If the farmer kept the coat on and rushed to pay without any haggling, then Teitelbaum knew that the magic had worked. Some of the peasants were convinced they'd find something even bigger in Teitelbaum's money coat, a real fortune, like a little sack of gold or silver sewn into the hem, or at least a hidden envelope stuffed with a few thousand zlotys.

"It's a wonder that the trick didn't get out, but none of the farmers ever breathed a word. They would have been too ashamed at letting themselves be duped like that, because the bills Teitelbaum hid in the pocket weren't really worth very much—in any case much less than what they might have saved by haggling with Teitelbaum, if they'd only kept their heads while they were buying the coat.

"So Teitelbaum could keep on finding new farmers for his coats. Of course he did have to make sure he remembered their faces, so he wouldn't try to trick the same person twice. Otherwise they'd try on the coat, take the few zlotys out of the pocket, and run off without buying a thing. And Teitelbaum could hardly chase after them to accuse them of theft.

"You know how I found out about the magic coat? Just before the invasion, Poldek and Samek let me in on the secret. Teitelbaum had stopped hiring them, so naturally they didn't have much good to say about him. Their whole family was so poor that they walked with their heads bowed—but not out of shame so much as need, in the hope of finding a small coin on the ground or something useful that a person with a full stomach had overlooked. And whatever they found, they put to use, whether it was a piece of iron, a cigarette stub, or an old rag someone had carelessly tossed away. Poldek's redheaded daughter, Leah Dresel, also walked with her eyes down, but that was only because she didn't realize it was possible to go through the streets any other way. And her four brothers and all her cousins followed her lead, since she was the oldest, and it was her job to teach them the important things in life. So you could always spot a Teitelbaum from a distance, and even later on, when they came into some money—although that only lasted a little while—they still kept their heads down, simply out of habit."

Mrs. Kugelman shifts in her chair and I realize that against all expectation I'm actually moved by what she has to say.

"Every morning," she goes on, "on the way to our high school, I used to run into Leah Dresel with her flaming red hair. She and her two younger sisters went to Beis Yaakov, a school for pious girls, which had been founded by the great philanthropist Yoyne Breitschwanz. He was a butcher who'd made a fortune on sausage. He had fifteen children who all turned out well and helped him cure the thick sausages. He donated the top floor of his sausage factory for the religious girls to study. But those girls must have been pretty tough, if they were able to study in a building where the basement was running with the blood of slaughtered animals. I shuddered every time our paths crossed.

"You won't believe who we had to thank for our own school: a brother and sister who didn't turn out so well. Their father, Abraham Fürstenberg, was far and away the richest and most powerful factory owner in town. People called him a *sheyne yid*, a lovely Jew, because even though he was bald and fat he was such charitable man, a *maecenas*, a man of good deeds. Every fall after Sukkoth he'd have a quarter ton of coal delivered from his mine to all the town's organizations, whether religious or not—enough to take care of their heating for almost the whole winter. That's what a generous man he was. He always had a checked handkerchief on hand to wipe his eyes, which were constantly

red and tearing, but never failed to spot a good bargain.
Fürstenberg specialized in buying run-down factories.
He would leave his chauffeur behind and drive his dark
blue limousine to whatever place he was looking at. There
he would climb out of the car, inspect the buildings from
the outside, then go inside and pay careful attention to his
eyes. If his eyes stopped tearing, then he knew that the
dilapidated factory could be a real gold mine that would
bring work and bread to the poor, prosperity to Będzin,
and make Fürstenberg even richer than he already was. So
he would buy it on the spot from the baffled owner.

"Fürstenberg was a man of vision, dedicated to raising a
new generation of Jews. He loved the idea of taking poor
children and turning them into upstanding, progressive
Jewish citizens. But no amount of threats or punishments
worked with his own children. They brought him nothing
but bitter, painful disappointment. He was unable to make
a decent Jew out of his lazy son, Shlomo, who drank vodka,
played cards, slept all day, and only came to life at night.
And he was appalled when his daughter, Gutka, a kind,
sensitive girl who had always given him much joy, married
a Christian, and a mere laborer at that—a packer in Fürstenberg's varnish factory. After that she was banished from
her parents' fine home.

"But Fürstenberg wasn't about to let his wayward children ruin his dream. He disowned them and donated part
of his fortune to our school, which had been called the
Yavne Academy but was now renamed after its new bene-
factor. Nothing like the old-fashioned religious schools,

the Fürstenberg Gymnasium was secular and modern and dedicated to progress. In return, almost as a punishment, it was located on the top floor of a badly run-down building, in rooms that were so old, ugly, and unhygienic that we students were horrified. But we did have our share of fun in the morning, because there was an entertaining spectacle on every floor. On the second story we could see Solly Maiteles teach ballroom dancing to the Będzin servant girls. They came to him on their day off and paid a few pennies to learn how to dance. Maiteles, a scrawny man with flowing white hair, acted like the strictest schoolmaster, but if you came closer you could see that his eyes were full of fear—the fear of a hunted man. He wore his large hat slanted across his forehead to hide his powdered face. And if you looked carefully you could make out a few flounces on his pant legs, which we really liked. Of course back then we had no idea what we were seeing.

"The third floor housed the Hakoach sport club, which all the students revered and dreamed of joining. For the time being, though, we were only allowed in for gymnastics class. The floor above that belonged to the cobblers and tailors, and we always liked to watch them at work, right up to the morning bell. Sometimes, if they weren't too busy, they'd let us pull a needle through a scrap of cloth.

"Fürstenberg believed that the Yavne pupils would never become good modern Jews in that kind of environment. And because their bodies needed to develop as freely as their minds, he built them a magnificent schoolhouse— four stories high, full of light, with large windows, a spacious yard, and an inviting game field. It was the most modern building in town, which filled us with pride. We called it our kingdom, and Fürstenberg was the king. To show our respect, we always used the side entrance, while our honored teachers and esteemed principal stepped into their realm like true aristocrats, through the elegantly curved glass doors in front."

"Oh, come on, Mrs. Kugelman," I interrupt her. "Are you telling me you never used the front entrance?"

She glares at me. Fine, let her glare: is there something wrong with asking a question? Besides, this is my room and I can do whatever I please.

"Never," she answers indignantly. "We worshipped our teachers. Practically every single one of them had studied in Galicia, and that was our great intellectual center. We always addressed them as professor," she blurts out. I can see she wants to reach for her braids.

"So which of your teachers really did survive?"

"I think I better go now," she says, sounding offended. She gives me an uneasy look, gets up, and mumbles goodbye as she steps out of the room.

Clearly she won't tolerate any interruption that doesn't suit her. But I won't be muffled and gagged. She's stealing my precious time. I've made up my mind: tomorrow I just won't let her in. I get up to see if she's lurking about in the hall. Happy to finally be alone, I carefully lock my door and turn to my usual routine.

*   *   *

WHENEVER I STEP into a new hotel room, the first thing I do is study the emergency exits. I memorize my escape route, make careful preparations in case of a sudden fire, and practice for the real thing. I moisten a hotel towel, place it over my mouth and nose, and use a stopwatch to time how long it takes me to get out of danger. At one hotel I felt so thoroughly prepared that I actually wanted a fire to break out. I picked up the telephone and dialed the front desk to report a blaze. Following instructions, I did not panic, I kept calm, I activated the fire extinguisher, spraying the white foam in every corner, and together with the other guests I let the firemen rescue me from the balcony with the help of a swivel ladder.

At home in Frankfurt, I have a direct line to the fire department. Apart from that extravagance, I live modestly off a small inheritance from my late parents. I have good business sense but know my weaknesses, so I'm careful not to make too much money; otherwise I'd spend it on a bigger apartment and remodel every room but the bedroom into a kitchen filled floor to ceiling with double-walled freezers. Ideally I'd have seven kitchens, one for every night of the week, so I could follow my cravings wherever they might lead.

LATER THAT AFTERNOON I drop in on the hotel kitchen, pretending to be a diabetic with insulin shots that need to be kept in the hotel refrigerator. The truth is I just want to check out the freezers.

"You have a refrigerator in your room," says Daud, an

Israeli Arab who works in the kitchen. He has a big Adam's apple and wears a small earring in his left ear.

"Yes, but the shelves are too small and won't hold all my medications," I tell him. "I can't keep more than a day's supply inside my room."

He concedes defeat and lets me examine the refrigerators. Fish and meat have their own sparkling chambers, big enough to walk around in. The packages of frozen baby vegetables, however, have been relegated to an ancient freezer that doesn't keep them evenly frozen—and this shabby treatment breaks my heart.

"It's not really worth freezing vegetables, since the hotel gets a fresh supply every morning," Daud explains.

"So why the freezer?"

"We have to keep a reserve on hand."

"Could you please give me a key to the kitchen, just in case you're not here and I need to get to my medicine?"

"I can't do that, on account of the supervisor—you know, the kosher inspector. I'm not supposed to let anyone in the kitchen without supervision."

"Your kindness would not go unrewarded."

"All I'd ask is one small favor."

"And what is that?"

"Call me David. A lot of the hotel workers do that anyway, so they don't have to think of me as an Arab, even though I'm an Israeli citizen."

"And you let them change your name like that?"

"I do what I can to fit in. Otherwise I might lose my job."

What is it with this country and names? Next thing I

know the fake Silberberg will testify under oath that I've usurped her name and stolen her biography and that I'm trying to take over her life. Then I'll lose my ancestral name, they'll tear up my passport right in front of my eyes, turn me out of the country, and immediately before my departure hand me a new passport with a temporary name, only valid for six months, most likely the name of someone recently killed in a traffic accident, whose name was stripped clean of all blood and sinews just in time to be reallocated, because without a name of your own you can't pass through the border checkpoint at the airport to get out of this country once and for all.

Daud tears me from my thoughts. "They don't want to work with an Arab, so it's better if you call me David."

DURING THE DAY I stroll through the streets, taking in the city. In the evening, back in my room, I study an album I brought from home filled with images of frozen food, which are protected from my greedy hands by a transparent layer of colored cellophane. Ever since I started trying to control my habit, I've used these pictures to help combat any symptoms of withdrawal. All I have to do is look at a photo of something I crave, then I thaw it in my mind and fall asleep savoring the small, satisfying delight.

I wake up an hour later and take another look at the album, but there's no relief. The pictures accost me, ensnare me. I watch a package of beans free itself from the page and begin to grow. Trembling with longing I reach for the beans, but before I can get them into my mouth they melt in my hand. My hands freeze into a clump of ice. Snowflakes fall from the ceiling and in no time at all form a glassy wall of ice half an inch thick, behind which I watch, helpless, as butter-tender bits of vegetables float from above in a lavish display of abundance. As the scorching heat of the day begins to thicken outside my hotel window, I am in anguish, starving, cut off from all my favorite things that are ice cold and tantalizingly within reach.

3

━◆►

Skipping school

I'M STARTLED BY A KNOCK AT THE DOOR. IT'S MORNING, and Mrs. Kugelman is standing in the hallway, breathing heavily. She looks quite nice in her patterned sleeveless dress, smelling pleasantly fresh of soap, although I don't really like the fragrance. Mrs. Kugelman is sweating, flushed from climbing the stairs, her chubby arms flopping weakly at her side. She refuses to take the elevator, preferring instead to stagger up the three flights. The sight of her touches me. Despite my resolve of yesterday I let her in, but no sooner do I do so than I regret it. As she walks past me I notice that she's holding a raffia bag in her left hand, while in her right she has a plastic bottle filled with a chunk of ice, which immediately piques my interest. What does she have that ice for, I wonder. I can't stand having ice in my room; it will make me backslide. Does she mean to smash up the ice and shake the pieces into her mouth, smacking her lips while gloating at me with her round eyes? Then I'll see the pieces of ice flashing between her false teeth, and a consuming desire will rise within me, flooding me from head to toe, sweeping away my will-less body like a giant wave.

"What do you plan on doing with that bottle?" I ask slyly, ready to pounce and tear it from her clutches.

"In this heat you have to drink a lot. Didn't you know that? Every schoolchild carries a water bottle holder on his satchel. And adults drink up to eight glasses a day. I brought a bottle from the freezer so we'd have enough ice-cold water to last for a few hours while we sit here in peace and quiet."

"But there are cold drinks in the refrigerator," I say. "You didn't have to bring water from home."

"I know about the prices in this hotel. You'll be amazed when you find out, and then you'll be glad to drink my water," she says almost conspiratorially.

I stare at the bottle as she puts it on the table. The tattered label tells me that once upon a time, on some extravagant happy day, Mrs. Kugelman must have splurged on a new bottle of mineral water. But who knows how long ago that was.

Mrs. Kugelman fetches a tray with two small glasses that she sets on the table, and pours the icy mix from the top of the bottle. My glass fills with frozen beads. I refuse. "If I get thirsty I'll drink water from the tap," I say vehemently. She looks at me, unable to understand why I am so adamant in rejecting her fine water.

"You had your chance," she mutters, insulted, shaking her head as she re-caps the bottle.

I'm not going to be tempted by some ordinary glass of ice water. Even if she brought me a silver platter piled high with bite-size vegetables each wrapped in its own little icy sphere, I wouldn't touch a single one. I can't let anyone know that all I think about are shiny, rock-hard icicles—even though I really have broken my habit.

"I don't want to drink, I just want to listen. Please start whenever you like," I say in a friendly tone. I'm ashamed to have gotten the old lady mixed up with my problems and hope she'll forgive me for attacking her like that. Today I'll be all ears. What was that friend of hers called? Handsome Adam. Would I have found him handsome? I doubt it; probably I'd have looked right past him. I wonder who she'll talk about next. Maybe old man Fürstenberg founded an orphanage on top of all his other good deeds. What do I care about this town, anyway? That's enough, I tell myself, be patient, get a grip on yourself—after all, you can end these meetings anytime you want.

Mrs. Kugelman is visibly relieved at my lack of resistance. She finishes her water, leans back in her chair for a moment, then touches her chin and neck with the tips of her fingers and lets her hands wander to the thickest part of her blond braids. She twists them and twists until I slowly close my eyes.

"At the Fürstenberg Gymnasium," she begins, "there was one tradition we were especially proud of, and that was playing hooky. Each generation of students made sure to pass their collective wisdom on to the next: the secret passwords and hand signals, the best methods for sending and receiving notes, and the easiest way to sneak out of the building and slip back inside before anyone noticed you'd left.

"It all started back in the Yavne days, when a whole class of ten students lined up early one morning in two straight columns, just as if they were going on a school trip. On their way downstairs they waved to the cobblers and tailors; they puffed out their chests when they reached the sport club and peeked in at Mr. Maiteles's girls practicing their dancing. Then they stepped outside, as disciplined as if a teacher had been leading them, and marched right past all the stores and shops, right past their friends and relatives and in some cases their own parents. A few of the students went so far as to call out a friendly greeting. Finally they came to our little stream with its gentle banks and soft black water flowing as innocently as ever, with no clue that a whole class was playing hooky! The two students in the rear made a quick inspection of the area, and as soon as they gave the all-clear signal the whole group scattered and everyone ran wherever he wanted. Some went to the nearby asylum to catch a glimpse of the old man we used to call King Solomon on account of his gigantic beard, or to listen to 'Napoleon'—a hunchback who kept crowning himself emperor. A few of them just sat on the riverbank, enjoying the peace and quiet, and others played tag in the bushes. Only one or two actually went in the water, but they didn't swim any farther than to the opposite bank. At a prearranged time everyone met up and marched back into town in columns straight as rulers. And when they got back to school they acted as though they'd never left in the first place.

"Everyone skipped classes—good students as well as bad ones. Sly Gonna was usually the first to spot an opportunity, but he always waited until he saw that two others were thinking about it, and then he'd join them. Our class had an unspoken rule that no more than three students could leave at once. They'd sneak out during a break without making a sound. Some of them felt so sure of themselves, they'd swipe the class attendance book, take it with them, and then make it mysteriously reappear. Down by the river they'd think up new pranks, smoke cigarettes, and generally just enjoy themselves. For a long time I didn't dare leave the building, but for years I very much wanted to give it a try. Of course in my case no one would have known if I was actually skipping school or if the train I had to take from our little town of Zawiercie—where we'd moved from Będzin—was running late again or not at all.

"Anyway, I'd been watching the students from the upper classes for years and longed to skip school myself. And finally I did it. It was exactly a week after Purim—I remember the date so well because my little brother, Heniek, had been born several days before, and I remember how upset I was about that. I already had three older brothers and I desperately wanted a little sister. On top of that, the little runt was always in the way and always bawling and he'd completely ruined my grandparents' Purim party. So I was fed up and decided that it was high time to do what I really wanted, which was to skip school.

"I made my move right before the first class, just like I'd seen the older students do, before anybody could beat me to it. First I checked that no one was looking and then, quiet as a cat, I slinked out into the hall and climbed down the stairs and practically ran to the river the minute I was outside.

"Of course what I should have done when I got there was hide in the bushes, just to make sure no one else was around. But I was so excited, I forgot to do that. And the next thing I knew I felt a strong hand on my shoulder: it was my brother David, who skipped school all the time. David was one of the braver boys, known for pulling all sorts of wild stunts in the water, like paddling a rowboat standing up and rocking it until it nearly tipped over—but he always kept a watchful eye on the bank. Anyway, when he saw his good little sister Bella down by the river, he couldn't believe his eyes. He threatened to tell on me if I breathed a word to Father about where I'd seen him. That night, when he thought I was asleep, I listened through the half-open door and heard him tell our parents that one of my classmates had told him I'd skipped school and gone down to the river.

"With heavy hearts my parents decided that from then on I better spend weeknights at Mrs. Żmigród's pension in Będzin; they were convinced that their delicate daughter was skipping school because she was so exhausted from the long daily train rides. That meant I only saw my parents and siblings in Zawiercie on the weekends.

"At Mrs. Żmigród's I felt like an orphaned child who'd been abandoned by her family, and it wasn't long before I even missed Heniek, the little crybaby, who now had my mother all to himself. Two other young women lived in Mrs. Żmigród's pension, but I never saw them during the day. I was the youngest, and Mrs. Żmigród had no idea what to do with me. For her I was an annoyance. When I was at school, she'd rummage through the other boarders' rooms, crawling under their beds and looking through the wardrobes and checking every piece of underwear for evidence of some love affair. Every day I'd come back and find her covered with dust, short of breath, her eyes burning, and her ash-gray hair hanging limply down her back—furious that I'd interrupted her snooping. My only consolation was the freshly baked crispy roll with my favorite kind of eggs that my mother sent me every day through David. He took it on the train and delivered it to me during our first break. But he never looked me in the eye, and as soon as he handed me my roll he ran away as fast as he could."

4

The proud Polish girl

Mrs. Kugelman checks discreetly to make sure I'm still listening. I'll let her go on a while longer, but only as long as it's not boring, or else I'll lose my patience. I give her a patronizing nod. She shifts in her seat, settles back, and breaks into a broad smile that deepens the wrinkles around her eyes.

"I know it sounds ridiculous," Mrs. Kugelman went on, moistening her upper lip, "but with all her prying, Mrs. Żmigród managed to miss the juiciest love story that was happening right under her nose, because the boarder who was really in love was me. I'd fallen head over heels for the proud Polish girl. I idolized her, worshipped her. Then again, even if she had noticed, I'm sure Mrs. Żmigród would have chalked it all off to the confused feelings of an immature schoolgirl. But I was in agony: I couldn't make it through the day unless I somehow managed to spend time with the proud Polish girl. I did everything I could think of to get her to come to Mrs. Żmigród's pension as often as possible. And when she did, I'd secretly set back her watch, which she put on the table while she did her lessons, so that she'd stay an extra hour. I couldn't take my eyes off her. And just so she never got bored even for a minute I kept coming up with new things to keep her busy. When everything worked out, and it usually did, the Polish girl would stay until early evening, and that was more than wonderful.

"If some boy got too close to her, I'd cook up something to chase him off. I was particularly worried about my friend Kotek, because he was also in love with her. The first day the Polish girl showed up, Kotek took one look at her long muscular legs and was smitten. She was a good two heads taller than he was; she had deep-set black eyes, tawny skin, wild hair that came down around her chin, with thick shiny curls spiraling out in all directions, and two firm pomegranates under her blouse. Her hips were as sturdy as a bear's and she stood firm on the ground with two wonderfully strong legs.

"At first we called Chaya—that was her name—'the big Polish girl' because she was so tall and had come to Fürstenberg from a Polish girls' school. Later we shortened it to just 'the Polish girl.' Her parents called her Chayele. The Kornwassers were well traveled and highly sophisticated—true citizens of the world from little Będzin. They spoke Esperanto to each other and placed great faith in education, which they believed would bring all peoples and cultures together. The family was fully assimilated, and all four daughters attended a Polish school near their apartment. In Poland, you know, Catholics and Jews lived in relative harmony until the death of Marshal Piłsudski, and it was soon after that the incident with the scissors happened in Chaya's school. German class had been canceled, and the girls were assigned a substitute named Mrs. Swoboda, who taught needlework. Of course they hadn't brought their sewing baskets that day, but enough of them had needles, thread, and hoops on hand to practice their embroidery. Only scissors were in short supply. 'Which of you has a pair of scissors?' Mrs. Swoboda asked. The Polish girl always carried her scissors with her: they were silver-plated and beautifully decorated with roses—her cousin Motke had brought them from England especially for her. So she raised her hand and presented them to the teacher. 'I'm not touching those,' Mrs. Swoboda barked, 'I'm sure they stink of onions and garlic.' The Polish girl said nothing and put her pretty scissors away. Two months later Mrs. Swoboda was called in again, and once again there was a shortage of scissors—in fact Chaya's was the only pair around. Mrs. Swoboda went to the Polish girl and curtly demanded her silver scissors. 'I'm sorry,' said the Polish girl, 'but I can't let you have them, because today they stink of onions and garlic so much, I'm sure it would make you sick to your stomach.'

"From then on, the proud Polish girl decided she would be different from her classmates with their nice-smelling scissors. Her school had class on Saturdays, and on those days she made sure she was never absent or late, but she refused to go up to the board or write essays or answer questions. She would just sit at her desk mute as a fish. But then Monday would come, a new school week would begin, and all scissor smells would be forgotten. The Polish girl laughed and joked, and joined in with her class eagerly and cheerfully.

"In the end she wound up leaving the school anyway— but that was out of love and not on account of scissors. While she was on summer vacation in Krynica, which is a beautiful spa town, Chaya fell head over heels for Shmulek Weinreb, one of the older boys at Fürstenberg. Then she lost no time in persuading her unsuspecting parents to let her switch schools, and in three weeks she had her wish."

"'CHAYA KORNWASSER,' YELLED our math teacher, Mr. Rado, a few months after the Polish girl switched schools, 'when you're walking arm and arm with Weinreb after school everything works out right, but at the blackboard nothing seems to add up!' That made the Polish girl furious, but before she could say a word Mr. Rado banished her from his class for a whole week.

"Mr. Rado was as ugly as he was unfair. He had a huge nose that came bulging out of his face, which was very dark and all scarred up, and hair so thin it looked like someone had placed a faded wreath on his skull. His overweight body hunched forward as he moved from classroom to classroom. But when he began to speak, something incredible happened. His vibrating, captivating voice straightened him up and changed him before our eyes into a charming young man to whom we listened raptly until the bell.

"Mr. Rado was known throughout Będzin as a skirt-chaser. He flattered all the young women with his lovely voice, but schoolgirls were another matter. He couldn't abide us, and called us stupid cows, even though we weren't all bad at math; some were brighter and worked harder than the boys. Every morning he'd step into the classroom and call out 'cows to the side'—meaning that all the girls should sit together. At first the Polish girl was outraged and insulted, but after a few months she got used to it, because the alternative meant not participating in class, and that meant bad grades. None of us wanted that."

"IN THE END, Shmulek Weinreb wasn't as passionate about Chaya as she was about him, but he was clearly infatuated with the Communist Manifesto. And since our principal wasn't one to put up with Communists, he wound up getting thrown out of school that very same year—an event Chaya had no way of foreseeing. After Weinreb was kicked out, Chaya had a strange reaction, and for a while she started picking on people. She chose Kotek as her first victim, since he was always trying to win her favor. We called Yoel 'Kotek'—or 'kitten'—because he walked without making a sound. He seemed to glide over the surface; in fact, you'd have to put your ear to the ground to make sure his feet were actually touching the earth. Kotek couldn't take his eyes off the Polish girl. He spent every penny of his allowance trying to impress her; he even bought her

Ajax chocolate cigarettes. They were the most expensive, and even up close they looked like the real thing, but neither the Polish girl nor the rest of us paid any attention to him, because he was the smallest and youngest boy in the class. On top of that he was delicately built; his hands and feet were almost like a girl's. Even years later the Polish girl was too proud to admit that she was just like everybody else and only interested in the bigger, stronger boys—which meant the ones who'd had to repeat a grade.

"But Kotek was hopelessly in love with the Polish girl. He put up with her meanness; he was happy if she noticed him at all. And she knew that. She laughed at him and looked for new ways to make fun of him, and her laughter was malicious and cruel, as if she were showering him with buckets of jellyfish. He was so smitten, he didn't even notice when she finally stopped. The last thing she did to Kotek was tattle on him to Mr. Rado, who apart from math taught a special etiquette class for boys: how a gentleman behaves on the street, how to greet the weaker sex, the proper way to doff a cap and bow to a lady. One day Kotek ran into the Polish girl on the street and was so taken aback, he forgot to doff his cap. Right away she told Mr. Rado, and as a punishment he made Kotek take off his hat ten times in a row in front of the class. The Polish girl stood in the door observing the goings-on with great amusement, and with each of Kotek's bows she nodded majestically, like a queen. Rado didn't mind her antics because in the end he didn't really care: in his mind the school was there to provide boys, not girls, with a proper upbringing."

* * *

MRS. KUGELMAN LEANS back, sighs deeply, and goes on:

"Later on, when she was here in Israel, our stuck-up, freethinking Polish Chaya turned religious for a while, can you believe it? And you know why? She couldn't forgive herself for standing by and doing nothing to stop a crime she watched take place right before her eyes. It was during the last holidays we celebrated in freedom—exactly ten months, twenty-five days, and twenty-two hours before the invasion. Weinreb, who'd been kicked out of school, was back in Będzin to visit his parents. He had set up a soapbox near the synagogue, where he planned to harangue the pious Jews. The box was very rickety and he asked the Polish girl to hold it steady, since he was planning to deliver such a fiery manifesto he was worried he might fall off. Out of friendship she agreed to help. It was the end of Yom Kippur, and when the Jews came streaming out of the synagogue, hungry and thirsty after a long day of fasting, Weinreb attacked them. He pelted them with garbage from a trash can he'd brought along and called on them to stop being the slaves and lackeys of religion. The Polish girl was sorry she'd let him do that, and years later she was haunted by remorse. She couldn't understand why she survived while so many others, including Weinreb, died in the gas chambers. When she first came to Israel, the pious Jews used to appear in her room at night. They stood around her bed and looked at her with hollow eyes. They accused her of humiliating them on their last Yom Kippur before the murderers invaded. She became devout so they would leave her in peace. But after a while, once she was able to sleep again, she stopped being so observant.

"Many years later, about a week before Rosh Hashanah, the Polish girl complained that the pious Jews were back in her bedroom, but now they were coming to fetch her. Two days after that she fell asleep and died that very night without waking up."

MRS. KUGELMAN SLIPS into her shoes, clutches her raffia bag under her arm, says good-bye, and tells me she'll be back the same time next morning. I can't figure out why she's leaving so suddenly. Maybe she's making her rounds, going from one guest to another, telling her stories. Or maybe she's so affected by what she's been saying that she can't go on. I'd like to hear more about the Polish girl. Somehow she appeals to me. Interests me. No, impresses me. The way she stood up to Mrs. Swoboda, with that quick come-back. Good for her! How brave she was compared to me. The story made me remember an incident from my first grade, when I was the only Jewish girl in my class and this boy looked at me and called out: "Die a miserable death, you stupid Jew!" He was just old enough to repeat what he'd heard at home but too young to pronounce the words correctly. Back then I just froze up in fear and pretended I hadn't heard him. Keep quiet, stay close to the wall, don't stick out, my father told me before my first day of school. I was so scared that I made sure to follow his advice. And when that boy cursed me I hardly breathed; I just stared at the whitewashed wall and imagined it wrapped around my body, protecting me like a fortress. I wouldn't leave the classroom until long after the others were out of earshot and I was safe. But the Polish girl—she was courageous! I just couldn't understand how such a free spirit could end up being so pious. Was it simply out of self-reproach? And how pious was she, anyway? Did she shave her head and wear a wig, assuming she was married? Did she hide her beautiful legs under a long dress? What a waste that would be, and in the end her nightmares caught up with her nevertheless.

Sighing, I fling open the door to the balcony and step outside. The sea is spread out peacefully, almost motionless, a giant swirl of bluish green against the sandy shore. Layers of white clouds are piled in the sky. Tiny droplets off the sea catch the sunlight so that the air seems to glow. I feel a surge of envy as I watch a group of young mothers sitting with their small children, chattering loudly under the umbrella they've brought along. They offer their children cold drinks from a lovely red cooler; I can hardly take my eyes off it. Their lips pursed together, cigarettes dangling from their mouths, they pour thick, hot coffee out of thermos bottles into paper cups and adroitly open plastic cubes filled to the brim with round pita and oily salads. A late morning beside the sea: barefoot beachgoers idling away their free hours on cream-colored raffia mats; an occasional couple lovingly entwined; night-shift workers snoozing in the sun, trying to catch up on sleep; and, a little farther off, a cluster of homeless people. Closer to the water, sinewy young men play racquetball, tirelessly batting at the hard black rubber balls in the shimmering heat. More beach idlers are stretched out at the edge of the water, their wet glistening bodies half submerged in the warm foam of the gentle surf. I picture the Polish girl lying in the same water and wonder if she ever managed to feel at home here, whether thoughts of her old country kept her awake at night—the recollection of soft footsteps on freshly fallen snow, the taste of sweet berries in the dense forests . . . How much of herself did she have to give up in order to adapt to this arid thimbleful of land? How many customs did she hold on to? How long did she go on eating her hot Polish soup before the main course, or taking out her fall sweaters in September, simply out of habit, despite the hot climate?

A series of curt commands from a megaphone startles me from my thoughts. Police sirens rip through the placid air. I move to the balcony and stand there, petrified. What to do? Crawl under the bed? Scramble out to the hall? I only have a few minutes to make the right decision. My heart is thumping; precious seconds are flying by—soon, a deafening explosion will destroy this hotel. I crane my neck to see what the other guests are doing. All the balconies are filled with onlookers. They seem to know the routine; maybe I ought to follow their lead. But do I really just stay on the balcony to watch whatever's about to explode, or should I get out as fast as I can? The beach is cleared of people and the police cordon off a large area. Two curious teenagers venture close and are brusquely pushed back. A man wearing a mylar vest and pants directs a gray delivery truck with an open rear door onto the sand, then slowly

approaches an ownerless bag, which he attaches to the cab
of the truck using a hook and a rope. The bag is gently
tugged up to the paved promenade. The crowd steps back.
A narrow ramp is pulled from the truck, and out comes a
toy-sized remote-controlled gray tank descending pur-
posefully to the ground. From a distance of three meters
the small armored vehicle shoots a projectile at the bag,
which bursts into tiny tatters that fly up in the air. The
crowd scatters in seconds; the silence is unsettling. No
clapping, not a single word of appreciation. People crowd
back onto the beach and go back to whatever they were
doing, as if a film had been paused and then resumed. Get
on with life, act as if nothing has happened—those are the
rules of the game here. A lone policeman rakes the blown-
up scraps into a bucket, while I stay up on my balcony,
shaking, unable to keep my thoughts from running off.
What if the bag was just a decoy? That would make sense,
wouldn't it? One person leaves it on the beach as a diver-
sion and mixes in with the crowd while another slips into
the hotel while nobody notices. I can see the headline:
"Bomb Blows Young Woman to Shreds in Hotel Room."
And the story: An elevator boy's vigilance saved many lives
yesterday when he chased a suspicious character out of a
hotel lobby up the stairs and into a guestroom overlooking
the sea. There the man set off his bomb, blowing himself
up along with a young tourist from Frankfurt who happened to be staying there . . . Happened to be staying—of
course it would have to be my room, out of all the hundred

thousand hotel rooms in this city. And it's all the fault of that cold-blooded doppelganger. She took my room and now I'm going to die. How do I know I'm still alive, anyway? Maybe I'm already dead.

Very carefully, I touch myself. I'm on the verge of collapse. I step back inside and reach for the paring knife in the small fruit basket—a gift from the hotel. I open the refrigerator. Cold sweat beads up on my forehead as I carefully pry apart the ice trays that have frozen together and peel off a tiny flake of ice. Soothing balm for what I've just suffered. Surely I'm allowed one tiny chip of ice—after all, I barely came out alive. This isn't backsliding, I tell myself, it's an emergency. Am I responsible for the fact that water turns into ice at low temperatures? I'm not the one who magically changes rain into snow. I didn't create the icebergs in the Antarctic or the frozen lakes in the Urals. It's not my fault, I'm not guilty, and what's more, I have to ward off nature itself, which is trying to seduce me at every turn and is hell-bent on causing me to relapse.

Quitting is easy, child's play, a simple gesture and that's that. All I have to do is drop this treacherous little knife on the floor and walk away. And I do, after one little chip. I don't need ice, I don't want any, I never did. I hate ice. The mere sight of it makes me gag. I feel the nausea rising in me and am glad, because that means the desire is subsiding, disappearing. I grasp the knife firmly with both hands, break off the blade, and place both useless parts on the fruit plate. I take a deep breath; a great burden has been lifted. I'm out of danger, at least for now. My mood brightens.

I switch on the radio; I listen to the latest American hits, fling open the door to the closet, rummage through my things until I find my new swimsuit. One last glance at the mirror and I'm on my way out of the room, almost cheerful as I traipse off to the beach. Keep your eyes open, I tell myself, and take a good look around: you never know who you might meet today.

5

⫷◦⫸

Handsome Adam

WHEN MRS. KUGELMAN WALKS INTO MY ROOM THE NEXT morning, I'm lying in bed with a headache, recovering from being smacked on the chin by a hard racquetball. And the worst thing is that it wasn't even a come-on. The young man who hit the ball acted as though it were my fault for standing in the wrong place. He looked handsome, all worked up like that, so I let myself sink to the ground as if the ball had really hurt me. As he came toward me I could see how smooth and muscular his body was. He smelled of sea and lotion. He was clearly over thirty and wasn't wearing a wedding ring. As he picked up the ball his hand accidentally grazed my own. I was electrified, fixed on his smoothly shaven chest. He brushed the sand off the ball and playfully passed it from one hand to the other before going back to his game. He didn't even bother to help me up. I was at a loss, desperate. I probably should have cried out in pain. In this country you don't get noticed unless you scream your head off. But it was too late for that. I was so mortified that I just slinked away from the beach. I spent the rest of the day walking in the glaring sun, with nothing to cover my head, until I really felt miserable. By evening I was so exhausted I collapsed in bed, forgetting to lock the door.

I don't hear Mrs. Kugelman knock, but there she is. Tired and dazed, my shoulders aching from the sunburn, I signal for her to enter. Let her talk; I could use some distraction. Maybe she'll help me get rid of this infuriating headache. I yawn and rub my neck. Mrs. Kugelman watches me. She goes to the bathroom, comes back with a small glass of lukewarm tap water, and places it in front of me without a word. Thankful, I drink. She waits for me to get up. Then she unties the double laces of her shoes with the special insoles for flat arches, pulls them off, and places them in front of her chair so that she can easily slip into them later. She takes a large swallow of water from her own icy bottle, gazes thoughtfully at the fine track of sand leading from the door to my bed, and then launches right in.

"YOU KNOW, THE famous poet Bialik once came all the way from Palestine to talk to our students. He said we were wasting our time learning Polish history and literature. 'This is not your nation,' he told us. 'Your language is Hebrew, and your country is Palestine.' You could have heard a pin drop. The next morning Pani Kleinowa, our Polish teacher, snarled at us that Poland was where we were born, Poland was our home, Polish poetry was sacred, and she wasn't going to let anybody dirty its name. What was so special about Hebrew? Besides, Palestine wasn't even a real country. And anyone who saw Yiddish as a unifying language was beyond help, she shouted. Yiddish was a relict of the Middle Ages, no—much worse than that—a reversion to some primitive Stone Age, no—even worse—to the beginnings of man! Admittedly Pani Kleinowa was given to hysterics. You could see it by just looking at her face: her pale blue eyes popped out and her mouth practically bubbled with emotion. She kept her faded blond hair in a tight bun at the back of her neck and used her hands while talking, with her fingers widely splayed. Bialik's remarks had really set her off, and she vented her anger in her rapid, shrill voice. And she wasn't the only one; the whole town was bitterly divided as to which language was properly ours.

"Handsome Adam, who was my favorite classmate of all, shared Pani Kleinowa's views. He was a staunch Polish patriot, filled with a deep love for his fatherland. But he wasn't entirely sure which side his father was on, and he wasn't about to risk losing his allowance on account of some silly remark. So he took care to keep his opinions to himself.

"Our whole school was split on the issue. Fürstenberg and the other trustees—all rich, respectable gentlemen with modern views—were ardent Zionists. But Principal Smolarski—a thin, unapproachable man—came from the famous cultural center of Kraków; he was a doctor of philosophy and belonged to a conservative Polish party. The Polish authorities had little interest in educating a new Jewish nation, and Smolarski was forever trying to keep them happy while appeasing the local notables. He used different tactics to steer between the two sides and did what he could to make sure the internal affairs of the school stayed private.

"Once he sent us to take part in a political demonstration in Gdynia, where we joined a group of Polish students calling for greater access to the Baltic. Poland's little piece of land on the Bay of Danzig wasn't big enough to handle all the shipping of a growing young nation that hoped to become a great maritime power with colonies of its own. We all enjoyed ourselves that day, but Adam was the only boy from our school to really embrace the cause. He ran out ahead of everyone else, waving the red-and-white Polish flag. What a shining patriot he was, so full of enthusiasm!

"And nothing meant more to him than the national holiday on the third of May. Each year he'd put on his freshly ironed school uniform that fit him so well and march up and down the town with the soldiers of the Będzin garrison. When it came to military parades with music and horses and artillery, Adam threw himself in, heart and soul. Actually, now that I think about it, maybe just with half his heart, because once in a moment of weakness he told me that when he was very little, he'd been playing outside with some Polish boys, not Jews. From a ways off he saw his grandfather coming, a handsome man with a beard, dressed in silk, an observant Jew who followed the laws but hardly to the strictest degree. Adam was happy to see his grandfather, but his friends called out:

"'Come on, Adam, let's go get some rocks.'

"'What for?' Adam asked.

"'Are you blind? There's a Jew coming. Hurry and get some rocks to throw.'

"'No!' Adam cried out, horrified. 'No rocks! Can't you see that's my grandfather?'"

"I NO LONGER remember when I fell in love with handsome Adam, only that all of a sudden I lost interest in the Polish girl and focused all my passion on Adam. At first, whenever he was near I couldn't breathe. I stood there frozen until he was gone. An earthquake could not have made me budge. Even weeks later, I didn't dare look at his beautiful eyes. I was afraid I'd just burn up into a little heap of ashes under his mocking gaze.

"From the moment I fell in love with him, he became 'handsome Adam.' I chose that name because everything about him was so handsome, and no one objected—least of all Adam himself. To this day his eyes are every bit as beautiful as they were back then, even if I'm the only one who still thinks so. He's paralyzed now, from a stroke, but when he looks at me I still feel goose bumps and get very shy. And despite how weak he is, he knows what his bright sea-blue eyes do to me.

"He had beautifully arched eyebrows and boldly slanted eyes. And long, elegant fingers. His skin looked like the finest porcelain, as if his mother polished it every morning after he got out of bed, adding a bit of yellow so it wouldn't seem quite so transparent, and so his tiny veins were hidden from view.

"Adam was the most popular boy in our school. Apart from Chaya, who thought only of Weinreb, all the girls were after him, and the teachers liked him as well. I really loved him, though. I would go looking for him during every break, but he avoided me. The others would warn him: watch out, Bella's coming, even when I wasn't. But it was enough for me to be near him: what I really wanted was to follow him wherever he went. And that took some doing. Sometimes I'd have to jump this way or that just to tag along behind him. My schoolmates made fun of me or tried to point me in the wrong direction or mimic my movements. But I followed my heart and stuck to his tracks, or at least that's how I remember it."

"ADAM WAS FAMOUS in our town for his escapades. He was always running away from home on some adventure. Some days his mother wouldn't let him out of his room: she could sense he was plotting something. She knew when he was thinking of skipping school and would send their maid, Bronka, to follow him. So Bronka hid behind each corner and waited to see if Adam was going where he was supposed to go. Adam acted as if he didn't see her but made sure she was following. Then he'd play hide-and-seek, letting her catch sight of him, before disappearing and reappearing all over again. When he reached school he'd pretend to go inside and then run down to the river. Bronka didn't fall for the trick, though. She'd pull him out of a bush and drag him back to class. Adam had a knack for concocting mischief like that. And he could always count on his cousin Godel to go along with whatever he came up with. The two boys used their Saturday visits to their wealthy grandmother to steal money from one of her collection boxes to finance his biggest adventure yet. The blue metal boxes with the curvy Hebrew letters stood proudly lined up in her 'French' salon, stuffed with coins to help the poor Jews in faraway Palestine. Adam and Godel couldn't resist; each week they chose a different box, carefully prized the slot a little open with a knife, then removed the money with the help of a magnet. They'd bend the opening back into shape and carry their loot back home. They were so good at this that their grandmother never realized she'd been robbed. But Adam's mother began to suspect something was amiss, and she started insisting on going with the boys on Saturdays, so she could keep an eye on whatever they might be up to.

"Adam dreamed of going off to foreign lands to serve some just cause. He wanted to make his way to Abyssinia, to fight side by side with Emperor Haile Selassie against the Italian invaders—he'd heard all about it one evening when his father was reading the newspaper to his mother. But he wasn't going to join the struggle alone; after all, what are best friends and cousins for? And of course Godel was always eager to do whatever Adam suggested. Adam went so far preparing for battle that he bought a pistol from Poniakowski, the guard at the soap factory, for twenty zlotys, saying that he wanted to practice shooting in his yard at home, the way they did in the movies.

"Adam insisted on running everything just like a military campaign, as befitted the two young warriors. To finance the operation they would requisition money from other collection boxes, and of course they'd need to stock up on provisions, because Adam's appetite was voracious. Adam's mother had a feeling that her son was up to something, and on the same day the boys planned to take off, she ordered Bronka to lock the door as soon as he came home from school. But Adam and Godel were so excited about their campaign that they forgot all about the money and provisions and ran straight from school to the railway station, where they boarded the first train to Katowice. Luckily no one asked for tickets. When they reached Katowice they ran smack into Jacob Teitelbaum of the magic coat, who was making his third trip that year to buy new supplies for his thriving business. Adam introduced himself as the son of Jungblut the soap manufacturer and a classmate of Teitelbaum's daughter Marysia. He claimed he'd lost his wallet. So Teitelbaum gave him a little money for the trip back home. With that the two boys bought tickets to Żory, which was as far as the money would take them, and climbed back on the train.

"Just a few kilometers past Żory the conductor caught them. When they saw him coming, the boys ran to the toilet and tugged on the door to close it, but the conductor wedged his foot inside. He pulled them out by their ears and at the next station he shoved them off the train with a kick so hard that they tumbled onto the platform. From there they made their way on foot to Ustroń, where Adam had a friend he'd met on summer vacation, Henryk Feingold, whose father was also a factory owner. Adam told Henryk that he and Godel had a school holiday and were on their way to visit friends, and that he'd stupidly set down their sandwiches somewhere and couldn't find them. Henryk gave them a bite to eat, though hardly enough for Adam, and let them stay in his room. While everybody was asleep Adam snuck into the kitchen and stole a loaf of bread. He gobbled down practically the whole loaf, leaving very little for Godel.

"Early in the morning they continued on their adventure, marching through the woods and beyond. Along the way Adam kept making off with bread from people's houses: the fact that he was stealing didn't seem to bother him in the least. And then all of a sudden they were nabbed by a Polish border patrol and taken to a guardhouse. The guards checked the color of their eyes, noted their glasses and their school uniforms, and determined beyond a doubt that they were the two boys who'd run away from Będzin. The boys were brought to the police station, where they waited on hard wooden benches until their parents came to get them late that evening. As he sat there, Adam had plenty of time to mull things over. He and Godel hadn't made it to Abyssinia, and they hadn't actually fought in a battle, but that was all right: next time he'd be sure and plan things better. He didn't expect too severe a punishment at home, because his mother was softhearted and always quick to forgive him. School was another matter, though. But as it turned out, our teachers didn't even scold him; they were too worried he might take off again and this time make it across the border. So Adam both was safe from reprimand and could take advantage of his new social standing. His classmates considered him a hero; two of them even refused to speak to him for weeks because he hadn't taken them along to fight with Haile Selassie."

NOW I'M WIDE awake, bolt upright in my chair. I can't imagine being able to roam around like those boys in Będzin. Things certainly weren't like that for me when I was little.

"Mrs. Kugelman, I'm dying to ask you something."

"Make it quick. I don't have time for a lot of silly questions," she answers curtly, standing up to stretch her legs.

"Did it ever occur to Adam how terrified his parents might be when they realized he'd run off like that?"

"No"—and her eyes sparkle like they do every time she talks about Adam. "All he thought about was having his adventure. His parents just made sure the police knew, so that they'd be sure to pick up the two boys. No one really expected them to get very far."

"You mean his parents weren't that worried about him?" I ask, unable to believe what I'm hearing.

"Oh, children in Będzin were always running away on some adventure or another." A hint of mischief flits across her face and for a moment I find myself looking at young Bella from the Fürstenberg Gymnasium.

I would have loved to run away like that. But I could never have expected my fearful, postwar parents to put up with an Abyssinian expedition. They were incapable of imagining childhood adventures. They saw danger lurking everywhere. If I stayed in my room too long, they'd fling open the door to make sure I was all right. If I stepped out of the apartment even for a moment without telling them exactly where I was going, they'd start calling the neighbors. I couldn't go out on the balcony without announcing it first. The tiniest scratch meant I might die of blood poisoning. Cutting a loaf of bread with a knife, lighting a candle with matches, riding a bicycle—all out of the question, far too dangerous. I didn't dare ride a bicycle until I turned eighteen, and then I wheeled around our block with the pride of a four-year-old. Compared to me, Adam was as free as a bird. That must have been wonderful. The more I hear about his adventures, the more I find myself wishing I had grown up in Będzin. Which is obviously ridiculous.

"My brother David once ran away from home, too," Mrs. Kugelman goes on, sitting back down and reaching for her water. One more adventure story and that's it, I tell myself. After that I'll show her the door. But she's not paying any attention to me, she's already somewhere else, far away, lost in her memories.

"He ran away on Lag b'Omer. I can't say why he decided to take off on a holiday, but all of a sudden he wasn't there. My parents had the police search for him, and they finally caught up with him outside of Łódź, at a training camp for young people preparing to go to Palestine. The police told my parents they'd have to fetch him themselves, since David refused to leave and the head of the camp was backing him up. My father passed the tricky assignment on to my mother, who bought tickets to Łódź for the following day. I watched her pack food for the trip in a basket, cover it with a checked dishcloth, and put three red apples on top, my brother's favorite kind. So that left me to take care of Heniek, the crybaby, who started screaming his head off the minute my mother walked out the door. The only thing I could do to calm him down was stick my tongue into his little mouth, but luckily that worked right away and then he fell asleep for several hours.

"My mother found David camping on a small hill. She hid behind a tree and watched him for a while as he helped a young girl hand out rolls to their group. The minute he spotted her he started running, but my mother chased after him, grabbed him by the arm, and said, 'There's no need to run. If you want to go to Palestine, go ahead, but you should know that I'm going with you and that means we'll be leaving everyone behind and so your father, your older brothers, baby Heniek, and Bella will all have to fend for themselves!'

"That vision was frightening enough to change my brother's mind. Right then and there he stopped resisting and traveled back home with my mother. On the way he wolfed down the food she had packed for him."

MRS. KUGELMAN LEAVES and I go back to bed. It's not as if there's anyone waiting for me; I can just lie here and think. So . . . the Polish police as gracious helpmates to Jewish citizens? I'm supposed to believe that Polish policemen helped bring Jewish children back home, delivering them to their parents with a friendly smile? That has to be a lie. Some kind of fairy tale. From what I know, the Blue Police—named for their long, dark-blue coats—were nothing but a pack of wolves who worked hand in hand with the Germans to liquidate the ghettos. At least that's what I'd heard over and over at supper, when my parents were talking to their friends, and their word is enough for me. Maybe things had been more peaceful once upon a time, before—but I just can't square that with the picture in my mind.

Those gatherings at home were the only adventures I ever had. Night after night we were joined by crowds of characters: crooks and con men, freeloaders looking for a place to stay, and people just passing through. My parents took in anyone who happened to be in Frankfurt and didn't have a family of his own. Our home was like a shelter for transients: the whole world knew you could always count on a warm meal at the Silberbergs. We squeezed together; our dining room table had the extra leaf permanently in place, and was always crowded with people I didn't know clattering with their silverware and talking very loudly in many languages. No one paid attention to me; I sat there as quiet as I could, taking it all in, asking for second helpings just so I could stay up a little longer. When no one was watching I'd dump the food into a napkin on my lap and get rid of it on my next trip to the toilet. Between the appetizer and the soup the crowd would typically start to quarrel; when they got to the main course they'd be mak-

ing business deals and arranging marriages. And by the time
dessert was served the mood was generally one of recon-
ciliation. The apple compote, cooked with cinnamon and
lemon, filled their stomachs like heavy, sleep-inducing por-
ridge, and their voices softened. Then my mother would
rise from the table, as a signal that dinner was over. Our
guests would say thank-you and good-bye, pinching me on
both cheeks as they left. I would go to the bathroom and
pat at my red, burning cheeks with a cold cloth.

THE CLEANING LADY is knocking for the third time, very
insistently despite the plastic bright red DO NOT DISTURB
sign dangling from my door. She's cleaned all the other
rooms, she tells me in a hushed voice, mine is the last one.
Then she pauses a moment and hisses: "If all the guests
were like you, I'd never finish anything." To get rid of her
I open the door and say that she doesn't need to clean my
room. That does the trick. She smiles and says, "My name is
Chana," then eagerly hands me fresh towels as she brushes
past me, quickly smooths out my sheets, and places several
small white boxes with the hotel's logo containing soap and
candies on the edge of my bed. Chana looks at me expectantly, as if waiting to be reassured that I really don't want
her to do anything else. Then she quietly shuts the door.

I stretch in bed, yawn, and, still exhausted from the
night, doze off into a short, shallow sleep. I feel as though I
were in a gently rocking cradle, gliding off toward Będzin.
The town is wrapped in morning fog, so thick I can barely

recognize the silhouettes of the buildings. Handsome Adam and young Bella are beckoning me into the woods on an early autumn morning. I scribble a note for my parents: don't worry, I'll be back soon. But for the moment all I want is to be free. I'm so happy! I feel pure happiness running through my veins. We venture deeper and deeper into the woods and suddenly realize that we're lost. For hours we blunder about the forest, unable to find our way back. I wake up, bathed in sweat, enveloped in Mrs. Kugelman's persistent hoarse whisper. I am surrounded by her townspeople from Będzin; they refuse to let me go.

I throw something on and go out into the hall. I feel as though I'm carrying the whole town on my shoulders, as if the people of Będzin have slung their arms and legs around me to stop me, as if they were pulling me back into the room. Step by step I push my way ahead. It isn't until I pass through the glass revolving door out into the open air that I come to, sobered by the sweltering temperature. The heat pounds into my head like a glowing wedge, separating the times that have flowed together. Slowly I regain my senses. I didn't fly all the way to Israel to be kept prisoner by some old lady telling stories about her school days that may or may not be true. I came here for a purpose, and I'm going to stick to it from now on. I'll make my way to Petach Tikva to pick up my inheritance and nothing's going to distract me from my search for happiness. Aunt Halina is going to make sure I find it and never lose it. All I have to do is take possession of her suitcase and fish service and I'll be inside my happiness forever.

That afternoon I order a taxi. Still feeling jittery, I climb in the back. Without asking my permission the driver, Koby, picks up two other women. I barely listen as he tells me that he only takes good-looking women, that he'd rather have no fare than take women he doesn't find attractive.

"Are you married?" he asks me in surprisingly fluent English flavored with harsh, guttural sounds. I tell him I'm not, and he asks the young woman sitting next to him the same question.

"None of your business," she says.

"You mean you haven't found anyone man enough to satisfy you?" asks Koby.

"What, you think you are?" she snarls back.

Koby offers us cigarettes and candies. The last to get in was an older lady, apparently a steady client. Her husband won't let her take the bus because he's afraid of terrorist attacks. Whenever she goes out he stands by the window and watches till she climbs in a taxi. On her way back, though, she manages to trick him. She's not afraid of using public transportation because she believes her fate has been predetermined, and she loves to go bumping and rattling through the streets on a bus, looking down at the honking traffic from her elevated seat. Then Koby picks her up at the end of the line and drives her home. The voices inside the cab grow louder as the two women tell their life stories: it's amazing how easy it is for women here to pour their hearts out, even to people they've never met. Koby intervenes with his commentary. For the duration of the drive he is our protector, he says, our father, our brother, our lover, who will safely deliver any woman who places her trust in him to wherever she wants to go.

SOMETIME LATER I step out of the lawyer's office carrying the old suitcase and am enveloped in the dark, moist steam of the evening. The brown suitcase with the wooden chest inside is so heavy, I can barely lift it. I feel the calluses forming on my hands, my fingers swelling by the second. They grow so painful I lose my grip, and the suitcase starts to slip out of my hand. I can't let it drop; I have to hold on; I know I'll never meet the right man unless my suitcase of happiness is firmly in my hand. I'm dying to know which man I'll meet. Where will he be—on the beach? In the hotel? What will he look like? Will he approach me because of the suitcase? How will he choose me from among the thousands of women? Or will I run into him on the street and fall in love as if struck by lightning, like Mrs. Kugelman and Adam? Will I pounce on him and never let him go? How will I know if he's the right one? The suitcase won't help me if he's not. It won't flap open to warn me. I must stay alert: he could be the first man I see or the last. I hate the idea that I might settle for the second one when it's actually the third who could make me happy. Or maybe it's really the fourth and here I've already committed to the third. Or there could be two right ones, the third and the fourth, and I have to choose between them. But what if it really is the first one and I pass him by because I can't trust that happiness is so close at hand. Carefully, with my shoulders hunched, I look around. Across the street the first man I see is Koby; his taxi is waiting for me.

"I'll take you back to Tel Aviv, for half price," he says.

"I didn't ask you to wait. Why did you?" I protest half-heartedly, close to tears. It's too late: at this point I can't just close my eyes and pretend Koby isn't Man Number One.

"Where are you going with that heavy suitcase? You can barely lift it. Climb in," he says.

Without asking, he opens my suitcase before stowing it inside his trunk.

"Security measure," he says. "We have to be on guard. For your protection as well as mine. After all, I have no idea who gave you the suitcase."

Soon he's going to tear at my clothes, pull off my shoes, search my handbag, take my money, and try to convince me that the only way I'll be safe is naked and spread-eagled on his backseat.

Koby's cab is full of paperwork: he carries his book-keeping with him. During longer waits he retrieves his letters and bills from under the floor mat, and pens, pencil, and sharpener from the glove compartment. When I climb in he quickly cleans up and secures his documents with red rubber bands—canning jar gaskets—to the inside of the visor.

"Did you come all the way to Petach Tikva for a bunch of old silverware?" he asked.

"Yes," I say, "it's a fish service."

"If you like fish so much, my uncle has a little fish restaurant with pretty good prices. I can take you there."

"Take me back to my hotel," I command.

Koby lives in his taxi; it's his second self, the wheels are extensions of his limbs, the headlights are his eyes, the knobs and pedals his nerves. He feeds his car carefully with oil and water, runs his hand tenderly over the small dents or bumps, waxes and polishes the body, kisses the talisman dangling from the rearview mirror before setting out on his first ride of the day. In the back he keeps shaving utensils, a first-aid kit, a bath towel, and a black yarmulke for trips to the cemetery.

"We can toss that suitcase out somewhere on the way, if you like—you're obviously not going to pack anything in it," he says.

"It was left to me by my aunt," I protest.

"That's it? No jewelry or money?" asks Koby.

"No," I say.

"Then stop with the long face and come out with me tonight to the disco," he says, turning toward me.

I catch a glimpse of Koby's khaki shorts, his hairy crooked legs, and decide right then and there to spare my future children limbs like that.

Traffic in Tel Aviv comes and goes like the tide and floods the narrow streets. Koby weaves through the dense mass of cars: he turns into alleyways, races past the small shops with wares spilling out onto the pavements, threads skillfully back onto the main thoroughfare. Solar panels flash from the flat roofs as we drive past the white buildings of the city, which has something makeshift about it. Founded in the salty sea wind of the flat sand dunes, the original settlement quickly expanded, swallowing nearby villages and eating its way through reedy swamps until, much to the surprise of its inhabitants, it revealed itself as a mature metropolis. A loud, roaring city, without streetcars or subways, and where two-toned, dusty buses groan as they carry untold numbers of passengers back and forth, from one stop to the next. The only thing that suggests this might be the secret capital of a powerful country are the occasional broad avenues planted with ficus trees, which give just a hint of grandeur.

Koby watches me in the rearview mirror as I look curiously out the window.

"What do you expect?" he says. "We're a poor, young country, one of the youngest in the world. We're allowed to make mistakes."

"Are you saying that older, respectable nations should have more patience with you?"

"Yes," Koby says, smiling. "Now you're beginning to understand."

That evening I do go with Koby to the disco. After, a bright moon lights our way to the beach. We make a bed, packing the sand that still holds the heat of the day. We bury our feet deep under the grainy blanket and use my skirt as a pillow. Koby gets up a few times to fetch cool water from the sea and uses his wet hand to wipe the sweat off my feverish body as if off a sick child.

When he drives me back to the hotel the air-conditioning pumps icy air into the cab. For a moment I close my eyes, and the backseat is transformed into a chair-shaped block of white ice, to which my clothes stick so firmly I can hardly move. I run my finger over the ice and lift it to my mouth to steal a taste. Small, bowlegged Koby-children bounce on my lap and tug at my clothes and need to be stopped from licking and sucking at the icy bench their father made just for me. Koby pulls over to the curb.

"I have to tell you, I'm married and have three small children."

"What are their names?" I can barely get out a whisper.

"Na'ama, Tomer, and Halit," he says, with a loud, clear voice.

I don't know where to begin with these names, I think, digging my sharply filed and polished fingernails deep into the fleshy part of my thumb, to distract me from the pain that Koby can't be allowed to see. If I had just a small piece of ice I'd feel better right away.

"Hebrew names," I say.

"Yes," says Koby proudly. "The two oldest have the initials of both of their grandparents hidden in their names."

"But those aren't real names, right? I mean, you made them up."

"They're modern. We haven't been using the old biblical names for ages. Nobody likes them anymore."

"What if your children decide to leave the country. How are they going to get ahead with strange names like that?"

"My children are never going to leave the country," says Koby. He starts the motor, drives to the hotel, and lets me out without a word.

* * *

THE CONCIERGE CALLS me around noon the next day, wondering if I ordered a taxi, since two cabbies are waiting for me in the lobby. I race down the stairs, heart pounding. I'm sure it's Koby. He's fallen in love with me and can't stand going through another day without me. He's not married, it's all a lie, he was just trying to protect himself so as not to be completely at my mercy. We will have three amazing children together, each more beautiful than the next, with international, European names. God in his mercy will cross his fingers and the children will inherit my long straight legs, Koby's hoarse voice, his skillful hands, his wooly, dark hair, his firm lips, and the pretty gap between his teeth. He'll spend the next few days driving me around the country, showing me the places of his childhood. He'll take me to meet his mother. That's bound to be what he's thinking, too, because I see he's brought along his buddy who switches shifts with him on weekends, because he's going to be best man at our wedding.

"This is my younger brother, Eli," says Koby.

"Hello."

"Eli drives a taxi in Jerusalem."

"Do you have other brothers who drive cabs?"

"No, just Eli and me. He isn't married and is looking for a wife."

"What am I supposed to do about it?"

"I wanted to introduce him to you. He's looking for a woman like you to marry."

"He wants to marry me?" I ask, bewildered.

"See, he has the same little patch of hair on the back of his hand you liked so much last night."

"You're confusing me with someone else. There's another woman named Silberberg staying in a hotel two blocks away. Go introduce your brother to her," I say, coolly, and flee to my room.

THE ENTIRE COUNTRY is in a state of hunting fever. Countless offices and branch locations and residential districts are busy making matches. Even at divorce court the invited witnesses are secretly hatching plans for the next happy connection. Blind dates are continually being arranged; whole banquets are organized just so two people wind up sitting next to each other. The chosen candidates are praised, their virtues extolled, their pedigrees confirmed. In this way a woman who dyes her hair blond and has had her nose straightened and her chin fixed manages to come from a long line of beauty queens. A man afraid of flying who hasn't been on a plane since his military days turns into a jet-setter, and on the day that the president arranges for a member of the Knesset to meet a distant cousin of the commanding general of the Israeli army in the cafeteria, politics come to a standstill, all eyes are on fixed on her entrance, the House of Representatives is dissolved, new coalitions are formed, and Parliament does not resume proceedings until the happy couple is joined and thanks the president while reminding him that his national duty also obliges him to find a husband for an unhappy neighbor who lives on the floor upstairs.

Strangers approach me in a street café; one has an uncle
in Melbourne who hopes to marry before he turns forty-
five, another has a son who is divorced through no fault of
his own and has two well-mannered children. I am pursued
by suitors hell-bent on marriage: at the hairdresser's, in
the supermarket, on the street. The elevator boy wants to
marry me, the waiter on the beach, even the hotel porter
asks me if I'm single and whether he can introduce me to
his colleague from the night shift. Chana from room service wants me to meet her son; the lawyer who delivers my
inheritance asks me out to dinner. They're after me. Even
in my hotel room I am not safe. A friend of Aunt Halina's
calls; he's heard I'm in town, I really ought to meet his youngest son. At the moment he's in Canada on a business trip
but he'll be back in Tel Aviv any day now, a handsome man,
very tall. Would I be interested? I say I only like short ugly
men, preferably midgets. It seems as though I've come to
Israel to save the ones left behind—men who've been abandoned or discarded or divorced—to rescue them from their
disconsolate existence. All sorts of thin, lame, fast-moving,
violent-tempered men descend on me. The circle is closing, it's getting tighter and tighter, they're pushing into
my room, tying me up, chaining me to the walls with wedding rings.

I decide to take fate in my own hands and resolve to
choose my own husband. I buy a wedding dress and walk
down to the beach, suitcase in hand. I have everything I
need: the white rhinestone-studded boots, the bouquet,
and the sequined bodice shaping my waist into a wasp's.

My wedding dress is stunning, far too beautiful for just one night. The seamstress carries the tuxedo for my groom on her arm, thread and needle in hand, ready to alter according to need. The hairdresser, the cosmetician, the photographer are sweating away, waiting for their moment. I've slipped both rings on my finger, the rabbi has been summoned, the huppah has been built, the chair set for carrying the bride, the wedding cake, the menus, the band, the amplifier, the flower children, the entire wedding group is sitting expectantly on the roofed terrace of the beach restaurant. Finally I discover a man I like, but the closer I get to him, the more he backs away. All the men I approach back away. No man dares come toward me. I am the disenchanted bride who lifts her own veil. I am the woman no one wants, who has no secret, who cannot be conquered because she can be had. The woman who dumps out the baby with the bathwater, who turns everything into its opposite, who stands with her head on the ground. Please forgive me, my poor unborn children, but the suitcase in which I had placed such hopes isn't bringing any luck. I am not finding your father and without him I can't start a family. It's possible that he exists and that he's lying low until I leave for Frankfurt. Perhaps my double has already snatched him up, the false, bogus Silberberg, who wormed her way into my room and now is plotting the heinous crime of bringing my unborn children into the world with my stolen husband.

ALONE, I WALK down to the beach late at night. I lie down in the sand and watch the day slowly break over the roofs of the city, in shimmering bright red stripes. Will there ever be another man for me to lie here with? How much more disappointment can I take? Where can I find the courage to start looking again? The sun comes up; I'm so exhausted I head back to the hotel. I want to sleep a couple of hours before Mrs. Kugelman arrives. It's nice to know there's at least one person waiting for me. I'm happy when she comes in. I take her water bottle and help her to her chair. Better a children's story about handsome Adam than lonely tormented hours in a strange hotel bed. She can even tell me stories about her school if she wants, as long as she stays here with me.

6

Yankel, Mietek, and Moniek

"We left off with handsome Adam," I encourage her, trying to show her the way, but she doesn't hear me. Lost in thought, she tugs at her braids until I hear her voice, as if underwater:

"My dear Adam claimed that as a little boy he had enjoyed a wonderful romance with his mother that was marred only by his burdensome father getting in the way. He consoled himself with the thought that his father had merely married into his grandfather's soap factory as a poor young man—so it was really Adam and not his father who was the legitimate heir. Leon Jungblut had no idea his son was thinking such jealous thoughts, and even if he had, he wouldn't have paid any attention.

"Adam's father was highly respected in our town. As a factory owner he was cold and calculating, strictly focused on turning a profit, but when it came to the poor he was softhearted and openhanded. He was easy to spot from far away: a dignified, tallish man dressed all in tweed, surrounded by beggars who dogged his every step like a tattered court attending its elegant king.

"The Wassersteins, whose store was next to Jungblut's new factory, complained bitterly that the beggars—schnorrers, we called them—kept knocking at their door and asking for handouts. They told Jungblut he needed to put a stop to that. But Leon Jungblut refused to say a word, so the street continued to be filled with beggars on Tuesdays and Thursdays, and the Wassersteins refused to speak to him for a whole year, until they finally got used to the sight of the schnorrers.

"You see, Leon Jungblut viewed begging as a legitimate occupation, a profession with its own codes and customs, its own sense of pride and honor. And it's true, the schnorrers moved in organized groups, agreeing in advance which group would beg where, and one group never got in the way of another. You could tell what day of the week it was just by which beggars came to which houses. They mostly married among themselves, too, since it was unlikely that the son or daughter of a schnorrer would be accepted by a better family. All things considered, the future didn't look very bright for their children. If they had any ambition at all they needed to leave Będzin and seek their fortune in America or some other place.

"Adam's father didn't help only the beggars. He bought tickets from the people who ran little lotteries on the street, but he never cashed in his winnings, just to help them out a little. If they had to pay out all the winners they'd never have enough cash to buy new prizes and keep their families fed. He also gave money to poor fathers right before the holidays, so they could put something on the table, slipping the coins discreetly into their pockets. And there was no shortage of poor fathers. Most of the religious families had eight or nine children and few of the men earned more than a handful of pennies. How many cobblers and tailors could expect to find work in a town the size of ours? Adam's family even took care of a group of poor yeshiva students and fed them day after day, until it finally got to be too much for his mother, and she gave them money to eat elsewhere. Meanwhile, as long as the students were in the house, Adam had to put on a yarmulke when he got home, so he wouldn't hurt their feelings.

"One day Adam accompanied his father to the factory. No sooner had Leon settled at his desk than the first beggar strode into his office—a middle-aged woman named Malka Feiga, who had bulging eyes and a long, gaunt face and dirty, matted hair. Her wiry body was covered with stinking, tattered clothes and her feet were wrapped in rags. All she said was, 'Good morning—four.' Without a word, Leon Jungblut took four coins out of a locked drawer and handed them over. Malka Feiga quickly thanked him and left the room. He explained to Adam that she was the leader of three other beggar women waiting outside the office. So as not to waste his time, she always told him how many beggars were in her group. And she scrupulously divided the money with the others even before they left the building.

"Once, on a day that wasn't designated for begging,

Leon Jungblut left his factory and found Malka Feiga waiting outside the gate. She had come to ask if Jungblut could help her son Yankel, the oldest of her eight children, who was suffering a kind of hunger that no meal could satisfy. He was tormented by a restless spirit that gnawed away at him. Malka Feiga believed it was a hunger for education, but she wasn't sure.

"Leon Jungblut decided to help the gifted boy, and so Yankel joined our class. Just think about it—a schnorrer's son at the Fürstenberg Gymnasium! At first we didn't take to him because he was so much more mature than we were. It was like having a grown-up in class. Yankel was already working for a living. Every morning before school he had to make the rounds for the bakery, distributing rolls. In exchange he was allowed to keep half a dozen for himself, so his brothers and sisters would have something solid to put in their bellies. During the winter his hands were often frozen blue, so the teachers let him warm himself by the stove during our first period. After school he worked for Bennek's delivery service. In summer they delivered all sorts of things—plumbing parts for the builders or scrap metal—and in winter they loaded up blocks of ice cut out of the frozen lake near the brickworks and brought them to our butchers."

"WHAT WERE THE ice blocks like in Będzin?" I can't help blurting out, though I try to hide my excitement, asking in a quiet, controlled voice. "What did they look like? How long did they stay frozen?"

"What do you mean, interrupting me with a question like that? Why on earth would you care about ice blocks?"

"Were they rectangles or squares?" I ask sharply.

"The blocks were long rectangles we put in our ice boxes," she says, on the verge of losing her patience.

That's all I need to know; now I can imagine adding a tasty block of ice to my freezers in Frankfurt. When Mrs. Kugelman frantically begins twisting her braids, I bite my lip and resolve to listen closely.

"YANKEL TOOK TO school like a duck to water," she goes on, giving me a stern look. "He loved playing with ideas, as he called it, and the chance to use his hands for writing instead of hauling heavy loads was an enormous relief, a real blessing—no, more than that, Yankel had discovered the joy of the mind. He could read a poem once through and recite it just like that, even adding verses as though he'd written it himself. He was quick to grasp whatever he read, and was able to convey its sense with language that was both featherlight and poetic. Despite his abilities, however, Pani Kleinowa, our hysterical Polish teacher, didn't like him. She loved the romantic notion of a poor boy finding a new life when she read it in a novel, but real poverty was something else. She was offended by its stench. By the way, Yankel never wore a uniform; that would have been too much like putting on a Purim costume, and no one insisted on it, either. The school's donors would have happily given him a used one, or our self-help organization would have come up with something, but Yankel stuck to his tattered, too-short pants, to keep his distance from the rest of us.

"The other teachers shared Pani Kleinowa's misgivings because someone who thinks of school primarily as a place to relax and recover is capable of turning the entire system on its head. Once you start questioning the whole purpose of school, once you ask who it really serves, it's easy to see the whole thing as a great big game invented by grown-ups that the teachers are all pretending to take seriously. But it never came to that because Bennek had an accident when a heavy block of ice fell off his wagon and broke his feet, and that changed everything. Yankel was now able to rent the wagon by the week and save his family from hunger.

"Yankel could have stayed in school, of course, but that presented a problem. The donors were prepared to pay his tuition, since he was so poor, but they weren't prepared to support his entire family, and they realized that was exactly what they would have to do to keep the boy in school. Even Leon Jungblut had nothing more to offer. Perhaps the wealthy benefactors were all a little envious of Yankel's abilities, or resentful because their own children weren't as gifted as the son of a schnorrer. One way or the other, the school was happy to see Yankel leave. Still, Leon Jungblut never lost sight of his protégé and six months later discreetly bought him a draft horse when the old one died on the street, weak from disease and starvation.

"For the moment, the rest of us kept on living in our little world far removed from that kind of poverty. Later on, when we were thrown out of our lovely apartments and sent to live near the *rynek*, the marketplace—right in the middle of the poorest of the poor—I found out how miserable poverty really can be. Even then, however, people like us had a bit of a cushion. It took a while for us to lose what we had, but the people who were poor to begin with had nothing but their misery, and that increased drastically from one day to the next."

Mrs. Kugelman stares off into the distance and several seconds pass in silence. She seems to be drawing strength from other memories, and suddenly she's back at it, with renewed vigor.

"WE DIDN'T EXACTLY miss Yankel. At school he hadn't made a single friend; he always kept to himself, and insisted on sitting alone in the back and not sharing his desk with anyone. Adam and I sat one row in front of him. At first I used to turn around to talk to him, but all he did was nod his head, so after a while I even stopped saying hello. He didn't seem to care and I didn't mind, because I was giving Adam my full attention, even though I was constantly fretting that he might decide my love for him was nothing but a burden. I was afraid that one day he'd have enough of me and go sit with Yankel. So one morning in April when I saw that the bench behind me was vacant, I sighed with relief. That particular desk was very much in demand, though, and the minute Yankel was gone both Mietek and Moniek rushed to take his place. The four of us soon became friends and luckily none of us was told to sit elsewhere.

"Mietek was the youngest of our foursome. Everybody

liked him at school, but things weren't so easy at home, which is why we called him a poor devil—I can't remember who came up with the nickname, but it fit. Mietek lived in the middle section of an apartment building that had a dreary courtyard, and the boys from the poor rear section hated him. Especially the redheaded Teitelbaum brothers, who chased him and teased him, calling out: '*Shaibele broyt, shaibele broyt*'—slice of bread, slice of bread. Then Mietek would run home as fast as he could and lock the door.

"It was true that Mietek was always asking his mother for a slice of bread. And he didn't know Yiddish like the boys in the courtyard, because his family had only recently come from Hannover, where they spoke German. They'd moved to Będzin to be near Mietek's grandparents, who owned two of the better apartments in the front of the building.

"Mietek's father was an ardent Zionist who had wanted to emigrate to Palestine, but the rabbi in Hannover told him to put off the idea until Mietek's little sisters were old enough to tolerate the hot climate. So Mietek's father decided they'd be better off spending those years in his hometown of Będzin, which he had left at the age of fifteen, and the family packed their things and moved there.

"Mietek enrolled in our school, and thanks to the hysterical Pani Kleinowa he wound up getting slapped by his father for the first time in his life, so hard that his cheek was burning for a long time after. The teacher had told his parents that Mietek would have to repeat the class if his Polish grammar didn't show immediate improvement. She was willing to ignore his accent, but she advised Mietek's father to speak nothing but Polish at home, so that Mietek could get used to the beautiful language.

"Mietek's father decided to teach him a very different lesson and slapped the boy so hard he went dizzy. 'Now that crazy Kleinowa wants to tell me what language I'm supposed to speak at home!' he yelled. 'It's not enough that your mother makes me speak Yiddish in the courtyard, just so they don't treat us like foreigners,' he screamed. 'Do you have any idea how much your laziness is going to cost us if you have to repeat a grade?' Mietek's father had no intention of begging the school for help—that would be a disgrace for the whole family. Mietek lowered his head and crept out of the room. He'd already caused his father enough trouble, and his grandfather, too.

"You see, Pinkas Dreiblatt, Mietek's grandfather, was a very devout man who wanted to send the boy to a yeshiva. When his son decided to send Mietek to the Fürstenberg Gymnasium, the old man flew into a rage: 'He's the only grandson I have and you want to make him into a goy!'

"'I'm not making a goy out of him, he'll still be a Jew, but he'll be different from us. He'll be a part of a new world, a Jewish state that will need engineers and doctors and scholars—not peddlers and shopkeepers like us. That's why he needs a school like Fürstenberg, so he can learn something that will help him get ahead.'

"The fighting went on for weeks before the two men finally made a deal: Mietek could attend our school, but every Saturday afternoon he had to visit his grandfather to study Torah.

"So that Mietek wouldn't be late for school, his father didn't make him put on tefillin while saying morning prayers, and he only had to say the Shema—only his grandfather wasn't to know anything about this. But the old man must have sensed something was wrong because he carefully placed a few coins in the velvet tefillin box. Early in the morning he took out his ear trumpet and listened through the wall to hear if the coins were clinking. After a few days of suspicious silence he checked the box and was horrified to see that the coins were exactly as he'd left them, clean and shiny, untouched by any hand.

"Well, that made Pinkas Dreiblatt so mad he stopped speaking to his son altogether, though the two men continued to share the Sabbath meal every Friday night. Mietek sat between them, trembling, not daring to open his mouth. His grandparents spoke among themselves, and so did his parents, and the two women talked as well. But the men absolutely refused to say a word to each other and used their wives as go-betweens, and then only if they absolutely had to. This standoff lasted for six months, until one Friday evening, when Mietek's grandmother was sick in bed, and without thinking, his grandfather asked his son to pass the salt. From that moment on the two men once again sat next to each other in peace."

"MIETEK AND HIS best friend Moniek shared a desk throughout their years at school. The four of us were always cooking up some prank or another and were often punished together, though handsome Adam did what he could

to get out of that. Once we were sent to the science laboratory after school and punished with extra assignments. I
started on mine like a good girl, but Moniek, Mietek, and
Adam began dancing such a wild tango with the skeleton
that the bones started to clatter. Then they played soccer
with the globe, the moon, and the sun, until the principal,
having heard the noise, came into the laboratory, doubled
our punishment, and thundered at us that he'd throw us
out of school. I was so afraid Adam would have to leave, I
offered to finish his assignments for him, and that annoyed
Moniek and Mietek, who had to work late into the evening, while Adam simply smiled, said good-bye, and went
home.

"Moniek was the fourth in our group. He was lanky and
scrawny, and had lively, shiny gray eyes that were full of
kindness. Guests who came to dinner at his parents' fancy
apartment were always surprised to see Moniek scooping
out the yellowish globs of fat from his soup and leaving the
meat in the bowl. To Moniek, the fattier the food, the better,
and he wouldn't come to the table unless there was some
kind of rich pastry crust.

"Looking back, Mietek and Moniek were both pretty
clever when it came to scientific inventions. They laid wire
and connected their homes with a secret telephone line
just in order to hatch new pranks. Once they played a trick
on Marysia Teitelbaum, who was the only child of Jacob
Teitelbaum with the magic coat. They knew that every
time she took her white poodle Kajtuś out for a walk, she'd
let him off his leash as soon as she was out of her parents'

sight. She wanted to give the poodle the kind of freedom she wished she had herself. But one day the two inventors lured Kajtuś out of her sight and colored his fur with black shoe polish or soot. Then they let him go and Marysia returned home in tears—with no idea—."

A KNOCK AT the door gives us both a start. Without waiting for an answer, the housekeeper barges in, mumbles the word "Minibar," and makes straight for the refrigerator. He checks the contents and restocks the little shelves with much clinking and clanging of bottles. He'll be sorry if he rearranges the freezer, I think. But he scurries out of the room before I can so much as blink, and Mrs. Kugelman and I are left looking at each other, bewildered.

"I've never seen one quite that rude, and I've seen more than a few," she says.

"Tomorrow I'll make certain no one interrupts us," I assure her.

"Don't bother. They'll come in anyway. They claim the guests never put out the DO NOT DISTURB sign as it is."

"Even in the expensive rooms?"

"It doesn't make any difference. They act the same whether you're in a tiny closet or the honeymoon suite," she says, shrugging her shoulders. Then she goes on.

7

◄o►

The Rapid Sports Club

"Elegant Marysia, Moniek, and handsome Adam all came from well-to-do families where money was never a concern. My own family wasn't exactly poor, but my parents couldn't possibly afford tuition for all four of us. Even with our special discount, school cost thirty zlotys a month per child—I remember exactly—enough for a entire family of four to live on. The factory where my father worked—in other words, Mr. Fürstenberg—took care of our tuition; he was happy to support the talented children of any of his employees. So even though we couldn't be called poor, I had to make sure I kept up my grades, given Mr. Fürstenberg's generosity.

"You see, if a wealthy child had to repeat a grade, it wasn't such a terrible disgrace, but a poor child couldn't afford to be lazy. In my family, if one of us failed a class, there'd be a lot of shouting and of course some form of punishment, but by the beginning of the next school year everything would be forgotten. However, if a genuinely poor student failed, which didn't happen very often, he had to leave the school right away, usually before the end of the year. The student would disappear overnight, after a painful meeting between his teacher and his parents, or a visit to the principal. None of us bothered to think about how unfair it was that poor children were never allowed to be lazy.

"As Adam's grades got worse and it became clear that he'd be kept behind, I stopped studying, too. I deliberately made mistakes in my homework and suddenly had no idea what to write on the blackboard. My own grades got worse and worse. If Adam wasn't going on to the next class, I didn't want to be there either, no matter how angry that would make my parents. That was before Yankel came to Fürstenberg, when I sat alone at a desk in the last row, right behind Adam, just so I could have a perfect view of his back. Sitting behind him, I could trace the delicate line of his neck with my eyes whenever I started to get tired, and that would give me new energy for the next lesson. No one could have driven me from my wonderful view. I was even able to bear my parents' great disappointment when they learned I had to repeat the class just like Adam.

"That was the same year that Moniek founded our new sports club, and the entire back of the class—including the founder himself, Mietek the unlucky devil, and my handsome Adam—were kept behind. In fact, we spent so much time building the organization that Moniek almost failed the same grade twice. He was the one who came up with the idea as well as the name—Rapid—after the famous club in Vienna. We organized our club into several different divisions, each with a president, secretary, and treasurer— one for the handball team, one for the speed skaters, one for the relay runners, and one for each of the other sports as well—and all this before our club had a single member. Our membership cards were stamped with a special seal and personally signed by the division president; we fixed up so many, you'd have thought the whole town was eager to join.

"Our first recruit was Marysia Teitelbaum, and her solemn admittance took place in the Teitelbaums' apartment, which had a large living room that the grown-ups liked to use for political meetings. Her poor poodle Kajtuś had to look on as his torturers handed Marysia her membership card, and Marysia was so thankful, she gave them a strong, heartfelt hug, with tears in her eyes because of the ceremony and the high honor of being the first member of the girls' division. Then, in front of everyone, she signed her card with her expensive Montblanc pen, very slowly, in her beautifully curved, perfectly clear handwriting.

"Our hearts had been set on joining Będzin's local Hakoach association, which was well known for its champion soccer team. We wanted them to take our entire organization, including our overgrown administrative apparatus, since Rapid didn't want to lose a single member! And we dreamed of having proper athletic shoes. But the only Hakoach team with decent shoes was run by working-class Bundists, and they all spoke Yiddish, which hardly any of us understood. To the Bundists, you know, our group belonged to the filthy bourgeoisie, and so the Rapids were barred from joining Hakoach.

"But the revolution didn't break out in Będzin, and when Hakoach held a grand parade to celebrate the town's new soccer field, the Rapids were allowed to march together with the other clubs, and we even got to wear the wonderful Bundist sport shoes—all because sly Gonna had the inspired idea to ask Stopnitzer the tailor, who made our school uniforms, to help us. He belonged to the Bund and was a champion of youth sports. Thanks to him, we were allowed to borrow the coveted shoes. They were very comfortable, handmade from the best leather by the Bundist artisans. Stopnitzer even took our boys into the Hakoach storeroom and helped them pick out the best ones.

"Wearing uniforms of our own invention, the Rapids were allowed to represent the various disciplines, performing athletic feats along the way, leaping and running and doing tricks on bicycles. Romek Ziegler, Moniek's hot-headed father, couldn't restrain his pride and shouted loud enough for the whole field to hear: 'Look at that! Take a good look! There, marching at the head of the parade! That's our future!"

"OUR FUTURE!" THAT whole afternoon I can't get Romek Ziegler's exclamation out of my mind. How clueless he was! And how horribly mistaken! I only hope he didn't have to witness the death of his own son.

What other dreadful truths are lurking behind Mrs.

Kugelman's description of her idyllic childhood? I find myself wondering just how much she's leaving out, simply to make Będzin look better.

The next morning, when she steps into my room, I pounce on her: "What's really so special about Będzin? Poland had dozens of little towns like that before the war, with parks and main streets. My father came from one. It couldn't have been all that different. He came from Kalisz. Do you know Kalisz?"

"Yes, I knew a few people from Kalisz who moved to our town," she answers curtly. "But you can't compare Kalisz with Będzin. Będzin was no ordinary place. The park alone was unbelievable, it was half as big as the whole town, and you should have tasted the ice cream we used to eat out of bright-colored bowls. The reason it was so delicious was because Süssmann the baker made it on Kołłątaj Street, and there was no baker in all of Poland who could bake *napoleonki* and *makowiec* like his."

"You really should stop making your town sound so perfect," I say, annoyed.

"I'm just telling you the way it was."

"You mean only nice things happened there?"

"That's the way Będzin was," she answers quietly.

"In other words a town where only angels lived?"

"Not angels, just Będziners."

"You mean to say there were no murders, no crimes, no hypocrisy or immorality? Did Będziners go someplace else to do their stealing and whoring and drinking?"

"When will you get it into your head that there isn't

anything bad to say about Będzin?" says Mrs. Kugelman, beside herself. "And if there were, someone would have to make it up." Then she stands and leaves without a word, slamming the door behind her. I pull on my bathrobe and run out into the hall, afraid that I've driven her away for good, but she's already out of sight, and I am left alone.

In any case, she really ought to tell the truth. She shouldn't pretend that everything in Poland was always happy. I want to hear the bad things about her city! My personal history of Poland begins with words like *judenrein*, ghetto, and cattle car. When I hear about a Polish soccer field I immediately think of an assembly point for deportation. If there's mention of a Polish forest, I see old foxholes, discovered hiding places, and summary executions. Was there ever anything else except the war? Did young Bella Kugelman really live happily and safely in her Polish town? If she did, then the safety was false, and would soon be punished by death! Cheerful stories from Poland? I don't believe it. I can't. No matter how much I long to hear something beautiful, something good about my parents' younger days—which they never told me anything about—I won't let myself be taken in.

I WAKE UP in the middle of the night in a state of severe withdrawal. I'm in such a rush I don't get dressed, just barely slip on my shoes, although I still manage to trample all over the picture album. Running out of my room, I check the emergency exit map for the quickest route to the kitchen. I sob as I open the freezer and in one motion sweep the packets off the shelf onto the floor. I bend to pick them up and press them against me with joy. The fierce cold almost burns my skin. Barely able to control of myself, I rip open the packages with trembling hands and dump their contents on my head, opening my mouth to catch beans, spinach, and baby corn. How I missed them, my icy friends. I keep biting and nibbling the vegetables until the hotel kitchen begins to spin like a carousel and I fall to the floor, unconscious.

The next morning I wake up in my room. Koby is next to me, comforting me. Evidently Daud/David found me at five A.M., at the beginning of his shift, surrounded by torn packages, deep asleep. He thought my blood sugar might have dropped; he checked my fingertips but saw no signs of pinpricks. Koby happened to be in the hotel waiting for a fare, and the two men carried me to my room. Visitors to Tel Aviv frequently can't bear the summer heat and go looking to cool off in all the wrong places, Koby suggests. Maybe I should go back to Europe and return in October, when the temperatures are lower. He says David promised to look in on me one more time and bring the coldest thing he could find in the kitchen.

When Koby leaves, everything around me grows dark, even though it's the brightest day outside. I'm lonely. Wherever I go, people stop their conversation. They whisper about me and turn their backs. It's been a long time since anyone really wanted to talk to me. My icy addiction shields me from the world but also keeps me bound. It controls me, compels me to do its bidding. Tonight I'll indulge in something that will make all previous experience pale in comparison: I'll bathe in floating sheets of ice, which I'll cram into my mouth and ears. And then I'll dive underwater for as long as it takes for gravity to pull me under.

The phone rings; it's the front desk. A lady has been knocking at my door. Am I available? I don't want to be disturbed, I tell him, I don't want to see anyone. Even if my doppelganger showed up to give me back my room, I wouldn't take it. I don't need it anymore. I'll give her the lucky suitcase and the fish service to boot. Of course, the first time she uses my fish knife she'll choke to death on a small sharp bone, assuming she hasn't keeled over already, while lugging the suitcase through the scorching heat.

Someone is knocking at my door, moving the door handle. Perhaps it's a nurse sent by Koby to give me a tranquilizer—someone trained in close combat waiting for the right moment to subdue me. Or maybe it's a welfare worker, some zealous American immigrant eager to lock me up in an institution. Or else it's another freezer fanatic whom Daud/David has given a key to the kitchen and who wants to join my nighttime prowling. She wants to sit down with me and figure out who's eating what when and which food we will share. I can't bear the thought of her shadowing me, of being stuck with her forever.

The knocking grows louder, and when I don't answer, Mrs. Kugelman begins calling my name.

"I don't have time today," I call back.

"Let me in. Think about Będzin."

I say nothing. What's the point? She knocks again, this

time even more forcefully, and then begins with her stories right outside in the corridor. Stories about the poor people of Będzin who went to a healer who pulled their aching teeth and cleaned their infected wounds and painted their throats with some pungent liquid—a healer who was just as poor as they were. And about a well-established physician named Dr. Goldstaub, who looked after the poor when they were very ill but took no money because that's just how people were in Będzin.

Stealthily I put one ear next to the keyhole, excited to listen despite myself. When her voice grows quieter, I open the door so as to hear better. Without skipping a beat in her story, Mrs. Kugelman pushes through the crack and into my room. She doesn't look at me, simply places her water bottle on the table, takes a seat, unties her laces, strokes her chin and neck, looks for the spot where her braids were once thickest, and moves her hands. I let her stories seep into me, warm me from inside. I lie down on the bed, fully dressed, sandals on my feet, purse in hand, ready to jump up at any moment if I sense they might carry me too far away.

8

◄○►

Dr. Goldstaub

"EVERYBODY AT SCHOOL KNEW THAT DR. GOLDSTAUB WAS the doctor who looked after the poor, but he treated quite a few rich children as well, including some from our school. He was actually a distant relative of ours. One time when he was giving me a shot he told me he was just scratching my initial in my arm so I wouldn't be afraid of the big needle. All the children loved him.

"Once Dr. Goldstaub even took care of Kajtuś, Marysia Teitelbaum's little dog, when he threw up after eating too many sweets. The fact is he treated everybody who needed it, except he refused to take money from the poor; when he saw what circumstances they lived in, he just couldn't ask them to pay for the treatment. He wasn't just being charitable, either; it was a deep, soul-felt compassion. Something we simply grew up with in Będzin. Maybe you could find that same feeling in other small Polish towns, but I think it was particularly strong in Będzin.

"In any case Dr. Goldstaub came by it naturally enough. The story was that his father, God rest his soul, was out for a walk one winter when he saw a horse pulling a heavy cart and shivering from cold. So even though he was a poor man himself, he took off his coat and draped it over the horse. We never found out how long the horse trotted down the street wearing the coat, or whether Goldstaub's father ran panting alongside the horse to make sure he didn't lose it, or when he decided the horse was warm enough for him to take the coat back.

"Kotek was especially close to Dr. Goldstaub, and not only because they lived in the same building; they were true friends. As a boy, Kotek was often allowed to watch the doctor at work in his kitchen, preparing medicines and leaving them to simmer on the stove. After the liquid had cooled, Dr. Goldstaub would pour it into little purple glass bottles, which Kotek carried to Gabłoński the Polish pharmacist, very carefully so nothing would break. Gabłoński was an educated man: conscientious, friendly, and short. With his back slightly stooped, he stood in his shop from morning until dusk. Mostly he spoke Yiddish, which he'd learned from his customers. He spoke fluently, with a good vocabulary and perfect pronunciation—not like a goy at all; in fact, if you didn't talk to him very long you might easily take him for one of us. He and Dr. Goldstaub were fond of each other. They enjoyed talking about chemical experiments or about the drops and ointments used for curing chronic diseases. Gabłoński also hired the doctor to prepare medicines for his shop, but that was mostly out of friendship, to help Dr. Goldstaub make up for what he lost from treating the poor.

"Dr. Goldstaub was not only a physician, but also a scientist and scholar. For the benefit of his patients he kept track of all the recoveries and deaths in our town, carefully recording all his findings. He was especially passionate about tonsils. He wrote whole essays on the subject, just for himself, and he was always trying out new medications to help ease the pain of the children in his care. Using a tongue depressor, he would peer into their mouths, turning their heads this way and that. Kotek, too, suffered from frequent severe sore throats, with aches and fevers. When Dr. Goldstaub saw the white coating on his throat, he told Kotek that it was a hilly landscape covered in snow with two dancing polar bears. Tonsils, he explained, were a strange sort of beast that got infected when children were sick and weak. Then they grew bigger and bigger until they turned into little polar bears, who came crawling out of their caves inside the throat and started dancing wildly. That's what made it hard to swallow. 'Now,' said Dr. Goldstaub, 'we're going to take some medicine to stop the polar bears and you'll see how quickly they'll go back to their cave and lie down.' Kotek would have preferred to keep the tonsil bears and give them enough room in his throat to keep on dancing. But he was very thirsty and it was awfully difficult to swallow. So he agreed to take the medicine four times a day and at last he beat back the bears.

"Dr. Goldstaub had keen eyes and ears and a perfect sense of smell. His ears were smaller than you'd expect, given how tall and thin he was—you could barely see them. Even so, they caught sounds too quiet for most people to hear, and he could make out several noises at once. If he'd have known how extraordinary his gift was, he might have become an orchestra conductor, but instead he chose to do without music, since the distortion from the gramophone was too painful for his sensitive ears.

"From the first hint of a cough, he could tell if the patient was in for a few nights of tossing and turning or about to succumb to some fatal lung disease. But no matter how quick the diagnosis, his resources for curing the patient were very limited. His two eyes were all the microscope he had, and he used them to uncover whatever was causing the rash or inflammation. He never missed a thing, not the tiniest bump, and the germs soon gave up trying to hide. He always started with the tongue, as if everything bad came from there. He'd make you stick it out as far as you could so he could observe if the coating was yellowish or pale green, and then he'd bend over and give a little sniff. You see, Dr. Goldstaub believed that every sickness had its own particular odor, even though some diseases tried hard to avoid getting caught, which made them difficult to figure out. In the rare event he wasn't sure about a diagnosis he'd take a swab with a little wooden pick and look at it carefully under a magnifying glass.

"Kotek claimed that Dr. Goldstaub's sense of smell was so sharp that he could tell at dinner what had been served on the plate the previous meal. Kotek thought it was sad that his friend had wasted his wonderful gifts on sick people when he could have been performing at fairs, amazing the crowds by telling people what they'd just eaten or, for a little bit extra, perhaps even predicting what they'd eat that evening. And Kotek would have loved running around collecting money in a big hat. He'd have happily accompanied Dr. Goldstaub that way for years, going from one fair to another. And unlike Dr. Goldstaub, he would have had no qualms about taking money from poor people—no, Kotek wouldn't have let the Będzin spirit of compassion bother him in the least."

"DR. GOLDSTAUB TREATED patients out of his home, and at one point he moved to Małachowski Street, the main street, where we lived. On Saturdays the whole town used to stroll up and down our street—that was one of our favorite things, but then again, there wasn't much else to do in Będzin. People would run into so many friends and neighbors that every few yards they'd be doffing their hats—here was Stopnitzer the tailor, there was Mrs. Żmigród standing on the corner, or Jacob Teitelbaum who was out with his plump, pretty wife and their daughter, Marysia, trying to keep Kajtuś on his leash. Or maybe Gutka Fürstenberg strolling with her Polish husband: much to her father's annoyance, she was not about to give up her Saturday promenade. Sometimes you had to wonder whether the men wouldn't be better off just holding their hats next to their heads instead of actually wearing them. But everyone felt it was a matter of courtesy and respect that they lift their hats and nod their heads at every encounter.

"Dr. Goldstaub didn't like those walks; the whole business of hat-doffing just bored him. He preferred to stand at his window and watch the people strolling up and down the street, noting how they greeted one another. He taught his friend Kotek how much could be learned just by closely observing people. You could tell how much respect one person had for another by the angle of the hat being raised in greeting, and if you looked carefully you could also interpret the response. You could see a lot in the course of a morning: various degrees of friendship or hate, and there were some pretty comic scenes as well.

"From his window, Dr. Goldstaub followed the feud between Donnebaum and Rosenholz, who had stopped acknowledging each other altogether. The two men had argued over a debt of a few zlotys, and neither had any idea who really owed what to whom. The feud then spread to the rest of their families, so the Rosenholz and Donnebaum children walked past each other on Saturdays without saying a word, holding their breath and stiffening their necks. But all might be well again soon enough. Dr. Goldstaub paid special attention to the children: if the Rosenholz offspring went running to meet the Donnebaums, he could be certain the feud was over.

"Dr. Goldstaub knew practically the whole town by name, and he could tell in advance who might be coming to see him, even before they knew something was wrong. With his trained doctor's eye he would watch how they walked and whether they were dragging their feet or hunching over and how often they had to stop to catch their breath.

"If Dr. Goldstaub had lived a just few kilometers away, in Sosnowiec, like many of our schoolmates who had to take the train each morning, he would have had a much harder time making his observations—because their main street there was nothing like ours.

"You see, Sosnowiec had far fewer Jews than Będzin, and while in our town both religions strolled together, in Sosnowiec the two groups kept to themselves. They walked at the same time, just on different sides of the street: Jews on the left and Christians on the right. Not because of any regulation, that was just how they'd done it for decades, and no one from either group wanted to cross the street and join the others. So one part of Sosnowiec, with its doctors, ironmongers, cobblers, tailors, and washerwomen, would greet each other on one side of the street while another group of doctors, ironmongers, cobblers, tailors, and washerwomen did the same on the other side—all under the very same sky."

9

◄◦►

Golda

MRS. KUGELMAN'S VOICE TRAILED OFF FOR A MOMENT, and I found myself closing my eyes, picturing the peculiar promenade in Sosnowiec. But she seemed determined not to let me linger anywhere but Będzin.

"Are you listening?"

But before I could so much as nod, she had launched back into her story:

"Dr. Goldstaub had a sister named Ria. She was very tiny and very delicate and went gray long before her time. Ria was married to Kuba, who was a distant cousin of my mother. They always came to our house for the High Holidays. For years they didn't have any children; then Ria brought a sallow, sickly girl into the world and named her after my grandmother Golda who had long since passed away. Dr. Goldstaub made a point of examining his little niece every week: he weighed and measured her and put her on a special diet of six small meals a day. In less than a year little Golda was transformed into a growing, thriving little girl, much to the joy of the family.

"Golda turned out to be a good student, and even Pani Kleinowa, our strictest teacher, who used to tear up your whole essay if you made a single mistake, had nothing but praise for her. You can imagine the shock when we learned that Golda was suddenly expelled from school. Here she was, a girl like you or me and on top of that a relative. But it's also true that Golda was a little different. Her eyes were jet-black and very alert, she had a pale complexion and a sharp chin, and she let her copper-colored hair hang down to her hips without so much as braiding it. She laughed loudly, coughed loudly, clapped loudly, and above all she was a very loud Communist who went around practically shouting that she was a member of the party. So loud that the principal couldn't pretend to shut his ears, and felt he had to respond to this provocation against school and country by throwing her out. Here our principal showed his sleazy side—he preferred to get rid of problem children before word leaked out to the authorities and they revoked the school's hard-won certification.

"Principal Smolarski was furious about how many Communist students had infiltrated our school. There were three or four who openly paraded their affiliation, and who knows how many kept their convictions to themselves, waiting until after they had their diploma safe in hand before they joined the struggle. He spent his nights tossing and turning and wondering if there wasn't a rotten apple—I mean a Communist—among his teachers. You see, the Communist Party was forbidden in Poland, and with good reason, too.

"So one beautiful spring morning just before Passover, Golda mysteriously vanished, but I don't mean that she was wrapped in a blanket and blindfolded and smuggled out of school under cover of darkness. The mysterious part was how suddenly it happened, from one day to the next, without the slightest warning, so that not even sly Gonna, her best friend, knew where she had gone. No one at school said a word, and the silence was more than obvious. It was as if all the students had conspired with Smolarski, and anyone who spread the news risked being thrown out just for mentioning her name.

"Naturally our class, too, was silent, even sly Gonna, whose friendship was so deep that each knew right away what the other was thinking. If Gonna's mouth said yes, even though he really meant no, Golda would immediately hear the 'no' thought and answer that. Of course there were lots of issues more complicated than yes and no, and the two of them spoke a language so secret, none of us could follow what they were saying.

"When she didn't show up at school for a day or two, Gonna assumed that Golda was sick. He went to her house and called out her name, but she didn't come to the window to wave the way she usually did. After she'd been absent more than a week, he sensed that she wasn't coming back. So one day he stayed behind in our classroom when they locked the door for recess. As her trusted executor he felt he was entitled to go through her things, and he found some newly printed leaflets written in the name of something called the Council of the Just. He took a few of these and stashed them in the class cupboard, so that some of her spirit would stay in the room. He also found a few cookies, a Polish-Russian dictionary, and a half-finished text denouncing unscrupulous factory owners, written in Yiddish. That would have been all well and good, if there hadn't also been a blueprint for staging a revolutionary uprising right in our classroom. Gonna didn't like the idea of dividing us by social class and standing—that would have meant treating some of his best friends as class enemies. So after thinking about it he tossed all the militant plans in the waste basket, where everything stayed peacefully in its place without going up in red flames."

"GOLDA'S PARENTS WERE forced to acknowledge that they'd raised a Communist, and that was a terrible tragedy. Golda was treated like an outcast, a criminal willing to let her entire family go to ruin just for her beliefs. For a long time her parents didn't dare show themselves on the Saturday promenade. They couldn't stand all the sympathetic glances, the showers of pity for having raised a criminal. Golda's carrying-on cost her younger brother Fishele his best playmate—Elias, Kotek's younger brother—because his family was afraid of her bad influence.

"And there was worse to come. Golda let her parents know that she had no intention of ever marrying or starting a good bourgeois family to take on walks every Saturday. Her father cursed her, threatened to disown her, declare her dead, sit shivah and say kaddish for her. It's a girl's duty to get married, he yelled. The only thing in the world meant to be alone is a stone, and if she didn't mend her ways that's exactly what she would turn into. For a long time Golda couldn't get that image out of her head. Especially at night, when business died down and all of Będzin went to sleep, it was easy for the mind to wander, and Golda wondered if she'd turn into a stone next year or near the end of her life, what kind of stone she might become, and whether she might be engraved with a hammer and sickle that would still show through, ever so faintly, after seasons of rain and snow—and whether a stone like that might not be more beautiful than all married people combined."

"AFTER SHE WAS expelled, Golda's parents sent her to Sosnowiec to live with her father's brother. Back then young Communists who'd been kicked out of school were often sent to another town, although that didn't happen on such a scale that we paid it much attention. Golda's uncle liked his niece with her hip-long hair, and he didn't take her political convictions all that seriously. In his mind communism would never succeed because people wouldn't be able to earn money, and money was all Golda's rich, well-fed uncle cared about.

"That uncle was a strong supporter of the bourgeois Zionist youth organization called Hanoar Hatzioni, and he let its members use his house for meetings. The rooms were very elegant, a thousand times nicer than the run-down

places where Hashomer Hatzair used to meet—that was
the left-wing group, designed for working-class children.
But because the rooms were so nice and because people in
Sosnowiec weren't so strict, a lot of the workers ended up
sending their children to Hanoar Hatzioni instead.

"Golda's parents hoped their daughter would enjoy the
meetings, if only because of the working-class children who
went there. But that's not how things turned out. When
the children showed up at her uncle's house, Golda couldn't
stop laughing. She sat on the steps, tossed back her hair,
and laughed her loudest laugh, which was much louder in
Sosnowiec than in Będzin, because there was no one to
keep it in check. It sounded like a waterfall, and with every
breath she gathered new strength for the next cascade that
came gushing out from deep inside her. The youth of Sosnowiec had never heard laughter like that, and it was con-
tagious. They started to laugh as well, and only then did
Golda turn serious. What's there to laugh about, she said.
It's time you woke up and read the writing on the wall. Palestine is a land without a future, these Zionist meetings are
nothing but a puppet show, all the dancing and singing in
Hebrew and all the brainwashing of little children does
nothing but get in the way of the truth. Jews will never live
in freedom except under communism, side by side with the
rest of the liberated world.

"In Sosnowiec Golda ran an underground Communist
cell and was in the process of setting up subcells when she
and her group were arrested. She was taken back to Będzin

and locked in jail without a trial—it was exactly one year before the invasion. The first thing they did was cut off her hip-long hair, then they placed her in solitary confinement, where she had to live in a dirty, damp cell separated from her friends. Golda was considered dangerous, and the authorities wanted to break her spirit, so every now and then they'd let her out and send her back to her parents' house, where she would wait anxiously, never knowing when the political police would come to get her and beat her and haul her back to the cell.

"At her parents' she would sit in her room after the midday meal, reading her old books. 'Golda,' her father cried in despair, 'when will you finally come to your senses and turn back into a human being?' She was moved by his shouting, since it was something she heard only at home—no one spoke to her at all when she was locked in her stone cell. There the guards didn't even yell at her out of pity, just to break the cruel silence.

"Back inside her cell, Golda would crouch in the farthest corner and stare at the bare stone wall, until one day she began to turn into a wall herself. Her arms and legs grew stiff, her face took on the same gray color, and bumps and bulges began to form on her head and legs, until her whole body was wrapped in a thick skin of stone. And slowly but surely Golda turned into a stone, just like her father had predicted. Whether or not daylight would have revealed the faintest hint of a hammer and sickle on the topmost layer, as she had wished, no one can say."

*   *   *

"SO GOLDA TURNED into stone, and the prison authorities forgot all about her. And that's how she survived the war, inside her tiny cell. When the Germans raided the prison looking for Jews, her name wasn't on any list, and when they looked inside the cell they didn't notice the little stone in the corner. All the other members of her group were stood against the wall of the prison courtyard and shot.

"It took a long stay in a Red Army field clinic before Golda finally came out of her stony shell. But her left arm stayed the way it was, hard as stone. Nothing could bring it back to life."

"DO YOU BELIEVE in fate?" I ask timidly. She stops and looks at me a moment.

"You mean Golda?"

"Yes."

"Well, her father's prediction turned out to be right," says Mrs. Kugelman.

"Do you think each of us has a path that's been determined in advance?"

"Yes, I do," she answers, very slowly. Her eyes fill with tears. "I survived the war so I could tell stories."

"And I," I say, laughing tentatively to brighten her mood, "was born so I could listen to you."

"You have to find your own path," she says drily, then stands up quickly, as though she's said too much. She smooths out her dress, turns to say good-bye, and offers me her hand for the very first time. Her handshake is firm, but her hand is small and fleshy inside my own. How warm it is. I want to hold on to it but she pulls it away. She tells me to expect her at the usual time tomorrow, and then she hurries out of the room.

What does Mrs. Kugelman mean? I pace up and down, wondering if that was just something she said or if I really might have some path of my own that I simply haven't found yet. What path am I supposed to find? And why don't I have any help? Even Aunt Halina obviously chose to keep me in the dark. Why didn't she leave me a letter at least? How am I supposed to understand the terms of her will? The more I try to figure things out, the more confused I feel.

I open Halina's suitcase, take out the old silver chest, and spread the knives and forks on the bed. Maybe I can find a clue. The mother-of-pearl handles are dull and dirty, the silver black with tarnish. Carefully I wash the utensils under warm running water and dry them off. I'm delighted to see the mother-of-pearl handles start to shimmer, and suddenly I notice that each of the forks has a fish finely engraved on the silver shaft. What a magnificent antique fish service! But what happened to the other four forks? And the three missing knives? Are they with the family of my future husband? Is the engraving a sign? Should I take out an ad calling all people with missing fish forks? Or does it mean I should limit my search to men with fish in their names, like Fisher, Fishman, or Fisherbach? Or maybe it's the name of an actual fish, one that swam alongside Noah's ark and was eagerly eaten by my ancestors?

I know how I'll figure it out. I'll use the eyelash trick. I'll put an eyelash on the tip of my index finger and start to blow while I think of as many fish names as I can. When the eyelash flies off, that's the name I'll start looking for. With my luck I'll probably end up spending all day in front of the mirror without managing to pull out a single lash no matter how much I jerk or tug. My own lashes will turn against me. In fact they'll lose whatever luster they have and thicken into gray steel rods that keep growing longer and longer, covering my entire face like some kind of medieval visor. And who's going to fall in love with me then?

No, I refuse to give up hope. If I'm fated to marry a man named after a fish, then so be it: I will find him. I have to concentrate, follow every lead, investigate whatever pops into my head. Who could have possibly had the silverware engraved? Who would have appreciated such a beautiful service? Did Halina bring it from Poland, from Kalisz? Were the Kaliszers known for eating their carp with particularly beautiful fish forks? Was Aunt Halina steering me toward Kalisz? What did that town look like, anyway? All I know about Kalisz is that, like Będzin, it used to be near the German border.

In the afternoon I finally decide to brave the noise and traffic on Allenby Street so I can find a bookstore with a map of Poland and locate Kalisz. Why did I never look up my father's town before? Why did it take Aunt Halina to push me?

I find Koby in a long row of taxis waiting outside the hotel and drive away with him over the protest of the other drivers. Koby is my private chauffeur and I won't set foot in any other cab. Today he's working just for me and won't be taking any other fares. I ask him to stop halfway down Allenby Street.

"Would you like me to wait? For you I'd even let the air out of my tires," he says, winking and searching for my eyes in the rearview mirror.

"No, don't wait this time," I say firmly.

"So you do find your father's town and then what?"

"Stay out of it, Koby. Your parents were born in one place and mine in another and they have nothing to do with one another."

"Except that both our parents' children are sitting together in a taxi here in Tel Aviv!" Koby turns around to show me he's scored a point.

"Where do your parents come from anyway?"

"Iraq. But I was born in Tel Aviv."

"You must have a large family."

"Yes I do," he declares proudly. "And they're all here." He swallows and adds quietly: "My family was driven out of Iraq."

"That's terrible," I say. "But at least they didn't go through the Holocaust."

"The Holocaust belongs to all Jews everywhere," he says matter-of-factly. Then he lists some cities in the Ukraine that lost their Jewish populations—names he recently learned from a Ukrainian immigrant who drives Koby's taxi on Saturdays. Koby has never heard of Kalisz or Mrs. Kugelman's Będzin.

He lets me out and coasts alongside me for a bit.

"Stop looking back!" he shouts through his open window. "Learn from us. Look ahead, to the future!"

He drives away, and I start to have doubts. Koby's right, I should turn around. Father wanted to forget his town. Whenever Kalisz came up at the dinner table, all he would do is give a quick, reluctant nod. Maybe I should just leave the past alone. No, I want to take a closer look, even against my father's will. I push on at a turtle's pace until I come to a shady street café well guarded by the security forces. Disguised as a thirsty tourist, I go in and order two colas at once. When the waiter has his back turned, I pour out the soda, fish the ice cubes from the glass, and pack them in the small cellophane bag I always carry with me. The ice cubes in my mouth console me; they give me strength. Not even the helicopter circling overhead or the ambulance racing past or the sirens announcing another attack can rattle me. With ice cubes in my mouth I am immune to fear.

In the bookstore I unfold an old map with place names like Lwów, Siedlce, Nowy Sącz—names I recognize from the guests who sat around my parents' table with my parents. In my head Poland is perpetually at war, and in the names of the towns I see death and destruction, empty streets, ransacked apartments, attics broken into to chase out the hiding inhabitants. I smell the fear, I see people running into the greedy arms of the szmalcowniks, the blackmailers who rob them. Here and there a lone saving hand, a sympathetic peasant woman, a humane landlord, a horrified nun, a lover hiding his beloved. What happened to all the stolen furniture, the hidden jewelry, the embroidered table-cloths, the abandoned silverware? After the war no peasant was tried for denouncing and robbing his neighbors. The mass graves are marked only by little hillocks in the fields, and the desecrated cemeteries—whose gravestones were used to fix up homes—are now refuse dumps. One man who passed through our house told how he went back to his shtetl Kamieńsk after the war only to leave it the same evening—after seeing the villagers wiping their floors with old prayer shawls.

The passionate love-hate that bound Jews and their Polish neighbors for centuries was torn into a thousand pieces. All I ever heard at my parent's dining-room table was a vitriolic hatred for the Poles that was far more intense than what they felt toward the faceless German murderers. I carry the germ of this double seed inside me. At the slightest breath of wind the seedlings run wild and spread their cold poison in my body.

I run my finger south along the map. Kalisz, Wieruszów, Częstochowa, Będzin. All towns once close to the German border. Surely there were dozens of small towns like that, towns that once orbited around the sun, nestled safely in the bosom of the Polish motherland. Kalisz is no more than 150 kilometers away from Będzin. But I don't know the slightest thing about my father's hometown. Not the name of a single street or neighbor. I have no idea whether Kalisz had salesmen who tricked peasants or rich philanthropists or whether poor people there went to a kind doctor who treated them for free. Were there families in one town who were just like those in the other? Did they have similar names? Were joy and sorrow equally distributed? Were Kalisz and Będzin like twin planets?

IT'S MORNING. I'VE been dressed and made up for hours and I'm waiting at the door for Mrs. Kugelman. I step out into the hall to greet her with a torrent of half-stammered words.

"Please, I don't want to hear about your friends from school today," I implore her. "Just talk about Będzin, what the city looked like, the streets, the trees—"

She cuts me off, offended. "Are you telling me what I can and can't talk about?"

"No, it's just that I want to hear more about Będzin the town, what the streets looked like."

"You mean who you'd meet on the street?" she says, without answering my question. "Why do you want to know that?"

"I just want to know more about your town."

"Are you starting to like my town?" she asks happily.

"Yes," I answer. Let the old lady think whatever she wants to.

"The streets were absolutely beautiful, clean, well-tended, and as children we were careful not to leave any litter on the pavement," she says, excited. "There were eight or nine big limousines, which belonged to the wealthy factory owners. They didn't drive by often, but when they did we'd stand there with our mouths hanging open. Of course at our age we were always outside on the street, along with all the peddlers, coachmen, and porters who made their living waiting for this job or that. We had enormous respect for the porters. Bachmans, we called them. They were very strong. I once saw a Bachman devour half a freshly roasted goose in one sitting, then wipe his hands on his canvas shirt, and after that wolf down half a loaf of bread. A meal that size cost four zlotys, but even if the Bachman only had two, nobody would have argued because nobody wanted to start anything with a Bachman. A Bachman like that could swing a hundred-kilo sack onto his shoulder just like a bag of feathers, or drink a whole liter of beer or vodka standing up. That's how powerful they were. One time they even defended the whole town," she says, then slips quickly out of her sandals and leans back with a sigh.

10

◄○►

The Bachmans

"When I say the Bachmans defended our town, what I mean is that they defended our honor. If a drunken Pole started calling us kikes and whores, all it took was a whistle and the porters would rush to our protection like a private police force.

"But the time I was talking about happened back in 1937. Groups of fraternity students from Warsaw and Lwów who belonged to the National Democratic Party—which sounds harmless but was really pretty awful—were going around the country picking on Jews, breaking windows and wrecking stores. They showed up in Będzin as well. They tossed their caps into the air and shouted: 'Hip hip hooray, we're here today, down with the pack of Jews!' A lot of Poles sided with them. Even Bolek, our caretaker's son, who was otherwise a peaceful soul, joined the rampage by showing the Endecja students where the Jewish families lived. On Kołłątaj Street the students ran into Mrs. Żmigród and her sister Rivka Sheina loaded down with shopping baskets, and amused themselves by chasing the two women toward the bridge. But before the students knew what had hit them our porters were on the scene, and a massive fistfight broke out by the river. The porters treated the students' caps as special trophies, and whenever a Bachman got hold of one he'd toss it high into the air, as a sign of strength. The students were at a disadvantage, since they were used to writing with one hand and doing nothing with the other, while the porters could punch away with both. A lot of caps went flying into the air that day and a lot of noses got bloodied down below. Just when they were about to surrender, the police intervened. They also fished a Bachman or two out of the water, which is how they saved Janek, a very young porter who'd never been swimming in his life. No one bothered to thank the brave porters: we took their help for granted. But the policeman who saved Janek from drowning was given a medal by acting mayor Pessachsohn. They really should have given him a promotion, because it was a bitterly cold day for a swim.

"One thing's for sure: after that the students gave Będzin a very wide berth."

"IN SEVENTH GRADE all boys in secondary education throughout Poland had to take a military training course so that the new Polish army would have a corps of officers coming from the educated elite. Our friends had to go through the training as well, even though there was little chance they would be conscripted, since the military didn't really want Jewish officers.

"So off they went: Adam, Kotek, Gonna, Moniek, and Mietek. We knew the Polish boys would beat up our friends, as a kind of initiation, and I was worried that Adam might get an ugly wound on his beautiful alabaster skin. But they knew what was coming and prepared. The very first evening they shoved their mattresses together, pulled some wooden slats from the beds, and waited. Just before midnight the attackers stormed their camp, but our friends beat them off. And that's how it went for several nights—an unusually long time. Fortunately my Adam came through without a scratch.

"When he got home Adam's father told him that Polish hooligans in Będzin had planned a pogrom at the exact same time and that they'd hidden sacks full of stones and iron bars in a large shed outside town, in the hope of breaking Jewish bones. But once again the porters were right there where they were needed, with their strong hands and powerful bodies, and the attack ended before it even began.

"I say porters but most of the time we called them Bachmans. Nobody can say why, though: it wasn't because there was some great family of porters named Bachman with strong fathers and strong sons that practiced packing and carrying wooden blocks in the cradle—they weren't actually related to one another. Maybe once upon a time there'd been a very strong porter named Bachman, and the name just stuck. No one really knew the whole story.

"Anyway, because they were very poor, they lived on the other side of the hill, near the cemetery, right next to the schnorrers. Housing there was very cheap, and the living space was crowded: more than a dozen people lived in two small rooms. None of us would have gone near the place unless we were desperate—even the grown-ups were afraid on account of the dybbuks they thought lived in the cemetery. But the Bachmans had no choice.

"People said that at midnight the dybbuks climbed out of the graves and took over the whole cemetery, leaping over the grave markers with no respect for who might be lying there and knocking off the little pebbles people left to honor their loved ones. And then they'd join in a wild celebration that culminated in a midnight dance where they broke the traditional separation of sexes that modesty demanded. Only the little children—and there were lots of those buried there—danced in a round all to themselves, right in the middle of the graveyard. But otherwise the dybbuk men danced together with the dybbuk women, the wise danced with the foolish, and the rich with the poor, though they were buried in different sections of the graveyard. Even the suicides, who were buried outside the cemetery wall, took part.

"The Bachmans were used to living with the dybbuks and got along with them in a neighborly kind of way. Each group took care not to bother the other, whether they were working or sleeping or pursuing their very different nightly pleasures.

"The porters worked hard throughout the week. But

they were pious, too. In the mornings you could hear them shouting at their lazy sons to get up and put on their tefillin. And on Shabbes they took off their peaked caps and went to prayers dressed in their good clothes, with such a light step that you'd never guess they spent the week hauling heavy loads.

"They didn't know how to read or write, except perhaps for a little Hebrew, but they did know how to count sacks and money, and they never made a mistake or charged too much. They were honest and had their own special Bachman code of honor.

"Once I saw them deliver ten hundred-pound sacks of sugar cubes to old man Dattelstrauch, a wholesaler who sold sugar by the kilo to smaller grocers who were too poor to buy a whole sack. Every family had to have sugar cubes for their tea: in Będzin we didn't spoon loose sugar into the glass and stir, we put a sugar cube behind our teeth and then slurped down the hot tea. That cooled the tea and the mix of bitter and sweet was delicious.

"Anyway Dattelstrauch always got worked up at delivery time, but that day he was beside himself. His wife—she was a very young and lively woman—had told him that she'd planned another vacation in Krynica and invited her parents, but of course without the slightest consideration of what it might cost. That put him in such a foul mood that he yelled at the porters so loud the whole town could hear. Even Jacob Teitelbaum next door forgot about selling coats for a moment and stepped outside to see what was going on. Dattelstrauch was fit to explode, he was yelling at the Bachmans not to break the sacks, and generally getting in their way so much it was making their work difficult. At one point the Bachmans had enough. They dropped their sacks outside the cellar and demanded their pay. But Dattelstrauch was already fuming on account of his wife's vacation plans and this was the last straw. He refused to pay the Bachmans the full amount. He claimed they'd been so careless unloading the sacks that a good percentage of the sugar cubes were bound to be broken, and so he'd lost part of his merchandise. The porters gave him no chance to reconsider. They jumped up and down on the sacks until the burlap burst. Then they bounced around on the sugar cubes that were strewn on the ground until not a single one was left intact. Dattelstrauch couldn't believe his eyes. The porters' boots had ground the sugar to powder and tracked it outside, like a shiny new carpet so thick you couldn't see the ground. The old man quickly paid the porters what they were due and even added a tip so they'd leave him alone. The Bachmans took their pay but tossed the tip at Dattelstrauch's feet. And even though their children were hungry, they wouldn't take so much as a thimbleful of the smashed-up sugar. That's how proud they were—and besides, for them it was a point of honor."

"SPEAKING OF HONOR: the Bachman code meant they weren't allowed to marry outside their own group. I know that for a fact, because one time it was put to the test. You see, the proud Polish girl fell in love with Janek, the young Bachman who was fished out of the river. He was so mus-

cular and handsome: strong and tall, with a head full of
thick black hair. He hadn't been in the business very long,
he was just a kind of apprentice, so he still hadn't devel-
oped the full sense of Bachman honor. Every Thursday,
when the proud Polish girl went to the market with her
mother, Janek put on a fresh burlap shirt. When she came
near he cursed as loud as he could, since he didn't know
any other way to attract her attention. His crude words
seemed to impress her, too. Then, to make himself seem
even more attractive in her eyes, he'd pick up the heaviest
thing he could find. Once when she lingered just a moment
longer than usual, he picked up a huge piece of metal and,
much to her delight, bent it with his strong hands.

"He liked her because she was so elegant, in her fine
skirt that showed her little round belly, if you looked closely.
Janek liked that tummy so much, he always made sure to
take his deliveries past the stand where the Polish girl and
her mother bought their groceries. And he liked her fine
manners even more. He heard how beautifully she spoke
Polish to her mother: Mamusia, look at this and look at that.
He loved the sound of her voice with its soft Polish melody.
Before long the two started meeting in private, going for
walks in isolated places, but in the end they were found
out, and the next day people were already talking.

"In Będzin the news made the rounds like this: First the
Polish girl was seen with the Bachman, which in our town
was bound to happen. Then whoever had seen them passed
it on, which was also bound to happen, and there was no
way an event like that could simply be ignored, not with a

couple as mismatched as this one. And once the ball was rolling it couldn't be stopped. The women spread the word on their way to the bakery in the morning, and the word grew as it passed from one woman to the next, doubling and tripling, swelling with details both true and made up. By the time the news left the butcher's it was so puffed up it couldn't fit through the door at Potok's grocery. So people talked about it outside, without bothering to enter the store. Some of them were so eager to hear it, they forgot what it was they needed to buy. Even the grocer stepped outside to hear what was so important and by that time what he heard was that a rich girl from Kołłątaj Street was getting married to a Bachman from over the hill.

"Before the gossip came to an end—because it always does, sooner or later—the news made its way to the parents. The Polish girl's elegant family had to hear second-hand that their daughter had taken up with a Bachman, without caring a whit for her family reputation.

"But she wouldn't budge, and in the end it was Janek who broke it off, and all on account of the Bachman code of honor. When the Bachmans learned the boy was going out with such a high-class girl, they beat some sense into him until he understood that a porter never set his sights on anyone from the other side of the hill, and especially not on a girl from Kołłątaj Street. The Bachmans made deliveries there and intended to keep on doing so. Work was work and heart was heart. Janek saw the error of his ways and from that day on he was a full-fledged porter."

* * *

"THE BACHMANS MADE deliveries all over town, especially on Thursdays, when everyone was stocking up for Shabbes. They also unloaded every sack of groceries, sugar, flour, fish, or meat that the farmers brought to the local market—it didn't matter that the farmer might be just as strong as porters or wanted to unload his cart by himself to save some hard-earned money. No, the Bachmans insisted on doing it; packing and unpacking goods was meant for their strong hands alone, because after all they had to keep their families fed, too. Not that the farmers didn't object now and then, but the sight of the powerful Bachmans stopped them from coming to blows."

"IF YOU CAME to Będzin by train you also encountered the porters. But first, before the train pulled into the station, you'd see two beautiful signs, the first with the word "Będzin" in giant letters, and then, just a little ways on, the word "Miasto," which means town. So it was the town of Będzin—to call it a city would have been too much, and "small town" would have been too little, and just plain Będzin would have been too modest. No, BĘDZIN—TOWN seemed just right. Travelers knew exactly where they were, and the porters waiting on the platform reinforced the impression of a bustling community.

"When Moshe Dreiblatt took his first trip to Będzin he had a suitcase like everyone else on the train, but it wasn't a very big one, because he wasn't carrying any wares to sell. He was coming to a bris for his nephew, Mietek's baby brother. Moshe's wife had stayed home, since she was very pregnant with her third child. So all Moshe had was a small suitcase with a nice suit, a fresh collar and black socks, his tallis and tefillin, a silver cup for the newborn, and of course some food for the journey since he'd traveled all the way from Nowy Sącz in Galicia. The suitcase was so light you could have easily balanced it on two fingers, and Dreiblatt wanted to carry it himself, the way they do in Galicia. But the minute he stepped off the train to greet his uncle Pinkas, he found himself face-to-face with two porters. Without saying a word they took his suitcase—and not in a friendly way just to lighten his load: they were enforcing the Law of the Bachmans. This law, which the Bachmans themselves had invented, applied throughout the town, including the train station, and stated that all packages and suitcases and other burdens—no matter how tiny—belonged in the hands of the porters. Once the porter had been paid—after all, what else were they supposed to live on?—the visitor could carry his own suitcase. Like all laws, this one had its limits, and it would never occur to a Bachman to carry the suitcase farther than the exit from the station unless he was asked to do so.

"But Moshe Dreiblatt didn't want to give up his suitcase. So the porters grabbed him instead, and gave his black hat a little tap—in Galicia they wear their yarmulkes under a tall black hat—so that the hat fell to the ground. Then they looked at Uncle Pinkas to show that Moshe Dreiblatt better learn how things worked in Będzin or else he'd be in for a very different kind of celebration than a bris. Uncle Pinkas quickly explained to his nephew: 'Moshe, give them your suitcase, I'll pay the few groschen.' Moshe respected his uncle and did as he asked. And so Moshe and his uncle followed the two porters as they passed through the station lobby, dangling the small suitcase between them. To the porters it weighed no more than a fly. It looked so light, it seemed to be carrying itself."

MRS. KUGELMAN HAS me spellbound.

"What were the porters called in Kalisz?"

"Enough about Kalisz!"

"Were porters called Bachmans anywhere else?"

"Don't be silly. Bachmans were only in Będzin, of course," she says loudly. Then she goes on with a dismissive gesture: "Probably they were called *pakntreger*—but I can't tell you any more than that."

Pakntreger! Now there was a word from our dinner table. I used to sit there quiet as a mouse and listen, although I only understood a fraction of what the adults were saying. So they were the Bachmans of Kalisz! I feel as if I were storming my parents' house, with Mrs. Kugelman covering me from the back so I could tear down the doors and breach the invisible barriers that always separated me from the grown-ups.

Mrs. Kugelman reaches for her sandals but I beat her to it. Holding her shoes, I beg her to stay. She looks at me perplexed and sits back down.

"What's got into you?" she says mildly. "You're acting just like a Bachman, and that's the last thing I need!"

"Mrs. Kugelman, I won't let you go!"

"Please put my shoes down. I won't run away," she says. She glances at the empty water bottle. I open the refrigerator and put out a row of little ice-cold bottles of mineral water, lining them up in front of her. I open one and fill a glass.

"Drink. Don't worry about the cost. It's a gift from me. Take it," I say.

Mrs. Kugelman takes a drink and fixes her gaze on me until her eyes cloud over and I sense that she's no longer in the same room.

11

Sly Gonna

"All the time the Polish girl was meeting up with Janek, sly Gonna acted as wild as a Bachman, even though he despised the Bachmans from the bottom of his heart and went out of his way to avoid them. He thought the Bachmans were all primitive people—when he was little one of them had kicked him in the stomach so hard, his rib ached for months—just because he'd gotten in the way while the Bachman was unloading a sack of coal. In any event, Gonna was so jealous that he actually spat right in front of the Polish girl, aiming high in the air so it landed at her feet. But that didn't suit his character at all, and it wasn't very smart, either, because the Polish girl simply spat right back at him several times and refused to say another word to him for the rest of the school year.

"His real name was Simon, but we called him Gonna—with a name as boring as Simon he clearly needed some kind of nickname. His classmates wanted to call him Spinoza just to annoy him, since he didn't like to let on how intelligent and talented he really was, as if he was ashamed of his gifts, as if his intelligence was a flaw, a disgrace, a cloven hoof. He was worried about sticking out, afraid we might consider him a know-it-all and turn away from him. At times he wished all the other students were as smart as he was, but there were also days he wanted to be as ordinary as the rest of us. Then he'd get angry at himself for having such a perfect memory. He couldn't help it, though—it worked all by itself, storing everything he saw or heard, like some kind of gigantic museum. Every now and then he even tried to trick himself into making a mistake, but never quite succeeded.

"One day Simon came late to class and I shouted out, 'Gonna!'—the word didn't mean anything, it just slipped out. Maybe I meant to say something else entirely, but there it was, and from that day on Simon was Gonna and there was nothing he could do about it.

"Gonna was our fastest reader. He was never without a book; he read standing up, he read lying down, he even read while he was walking. Three times a week he visited the lending library that Rabinowicz ran out of his grocery store. Our school didn't approve of that particular institution, since students were supposed to use the library at Fürstenberg, but we didn't like being told what to do and preferred to secretly get our books from Rabinowicz, even if it meant paying him a couple of zlotys in fees. The grocer was a doddering, gray-haired man who was as tight with his words as with his money. To get to the library you had to walk through his shop and go up two steps that led to a room way in the back. It was tiny, but when you stepped inside it was like entering a whole different world. Rows of books were squeezed together on carefully dusted bookcases, each volume numbered and cataloged. For Rabinowicz these books were the pillars of world literature; they were his pride and joy. He fretted over them when they were checked out, and laughed with delight when they were returned to their shelves. A few of us, including Gonna, had read through the entire collection and could hardly wait for a new work to arrive from Warsaw. Rabinowicz knew this, and did everything he could to keep us on tenterhooks. He'd wash his hands very thoroughly and then slowly unpack the brand-new book and hold it in his trembling fingers, leafing through the pages right before our eyes and sighing with appreciation. But instead of reading the book and passing it on to the rest of us, he'd place it in his display window for an entire month, enthroned on a pedestal draped with silk, as if it were some valuable rare gem. Each new book had an impossibly long waiting list, with all the names scrupulously recorded in Rabinowicz's tiny, shaky handwriting. But there was one person who didn't need to sign up because he read faster than anyone else, and that was Gonna. The new book always went to him before anyone else."

"AFTER HE GRADUATED, Gonna planned to leave Będzin to study philosophy in Palestine, since he couldn't expect to get into a Polish university because of the quota for Jewish students. You could count the number of places for Jewish students in the liberal arts on the fingers of one hand, and even in the sciences the authorities would bypass Jewish students to give the better laboratory assistantships to Christians. My older brothers had to sit apart from the Polish students, and one of Adam's distant cousins actually finished his law studies standing up.

"Gonna's energetic mother, Bluma, encouraged him to emigrate to Palestine and study there so he could have a better future. But she made him promise to become an engineer because the new country would need bridges and streets and machines—not people who went around philosophizing about the meaning of freedom. His mother also expected him to move in with his older sister, Halina, so she could keep an eye on him. Gonna promised to do everything his mother asked, just so he could get out of Będzin as quickly as possible.

"Kotek dreamed of going to Palestine as well. Of course, he was less interested in education than in getting away from his parents so he could play cards all day and gawk at the stars at night. In his mind Palestine was a Garden of Eden, a paradise where you didn't have to lift a finger. The cows milked themselves, the sheep shed their own carded wool, and the fields were a tangle of ripening vegetables all year long, golden ears of corn, wild herbs, and berries. Everything grew in abundance, and picking the fruits was sheer joy.

"In any case, it was clear that Kotek was very serious about emigrating. It was all he talked about, even lying to his parents that he wanted to study medicine. They tried to argue him out of going. His mother thought her eighteen-year-old son was still too much a child, that he wasn't ready to go off and live in such an unwelcoming place as Palestine. His father even offered to build Kotek his own textile factory, with a big office for the director and rows and rows of brand-new sewing machines. But Kotek wouldn't budge. When his father refused to finance his plans, Kotek paid a visit to Gabłoński, who owed his father a substantial sum for renovating the apothecary, and took the money home. Without saying a word he laid the bills on the table in front of his parents, as if to show that he could get whatever funding he might need. At that point they realized how serious he was, and gave up trying to stop him.

"Gonna and Kotek each applied to emigrate to Palestine, and each received the same forms at the same time. The deadline for enrolling in the summer term at the university there was April 15, 1939. But first the applications had to be approved by Warsaw, and before that could happen the boys needed to show that they'd graduated from high school. Naturally Kotek still didn't have his diploma, and how could he show what he didn't have? So he decided to put off enrolling until the fall semester and waited until July to send his papers—including his new diploma—to the authorities in Warsaw.

"Gonna was more clever. He very carefully filled out the forms and sent them all in before the April deadline—everything but the diploma. When the officials reviewed his application three months later, they asked him to send the missing document, and since by then he'd passed his exams, he was able to furnish them with his diploma. No one noticed the trick, and happy Gonna set off for Palestine on August 20, 1939, eleven days before the invasion."

"MAYBE THERE WERE other students who used the same trick. Maybe they saved themselves the same way, by moving to Palestine," I suggest hesitantly.

"Maybe. But who can say for sure?"

"Why did Gonna keep the idea to himself, when he knew how badly Kotek wanted to leave?" I ask.

"Gonna was different from us, smarter. We were still like children, but he was a lot more mature. It was amazing how thoroughly he thought things through. He knew the authorities would get suspicious if they received more than one application without a diploma, and he didn't want to jeopardize his own chances. So he didn't tell anyone."

"Did you ever see him again, here in Israel?"

"Yes. He'd changed enormously. He seemed completely closed up. I think he was tormented by the idea that he'd betrayed his friend for his own selfish reasons," Mrs. Kugelman says quietly and gets up.

I walk her to the door and as I shut it a thought twitches through me. What about my father? I feel dizzy. I gasp for air and collapse on Mrs. Kugelman's seat. My heart is pounding. My father was closed up, too. Did he betray his schoolmates just like Gonna? Was he also tormented by thoughts I had no idea of? I'll never know: everyone who might have told me something is dead.

* * *

ON MY VERY first day of school I had come home beaming, proudly swinging my new satchel. But Father took one look at me and his face froze up completely, his eyes filled with tears. For the rest of the day he didn't say one word more than he had to, he looked away when I tried to get close to him, he avoided me and locked himself in his study for hours. The next morning he stopped speaking with me altogether. We ate breakfast and he just sat at the table, staring forlornly at his coffee, without drinking a drop.

"Papa, we didn't get any homework," I said, disappointed. "When are they finally going to give us something to do?"

He didn't say a thing, just looked straight through me. So I repeated my question, practically screaming in his ear. Had he suddenly gone deaf? I tugged on his sleeve and pulled at his face, but he didn't move and wouldn't answer my questions. He refused to participate in conversation. My words hung in the room like thin shreds of ribbon. Father no longer heard them.

One day I took five coins out of the small pocket inside his jacket, which he always draped loosely over the chair at the head of the table. Since he wasn't giving me what I needed, I started stealing from him, but the truth is that he even encouraged me. The money in his jacket pocket that greeted me every morning was at least as eloquent as any conversation we might have had, and more dependable, too. Every evening he replaced what I had taken, so that in the morning I would always find new coins ready and waiting just for me, neatly rolled and pressed together.

Even when I started to eat nothing but cold food, Father still refused to speak to me. He doubled the amount of coins in his inside pocket and went so far as to include some really beautiful ones, in mint condition. At first I let the shiny coins slide through my fingers, but after thinking about it for a while I put them back. I didn't want to betray my newly discovered love of cold for a handful of coins, so I simply waited for my father to get used to my new diet. At some point he gave up. He stopped adding coins and went back to the amount we had silently agreed on and affectionately maintained. And I started stealing from him all over again, out of gratitude and joy.

My father and I sat at the table like deaf-mutes, while the guests carried on one animated conversation after another. He ate huge portions of meat that filled the entire plate. He loved sucking the marrow out of the chicken bones and chewing on the ones that had been boiled soft. He'd spit the hard, indigestible parts onto the middle of his plate with amazing accuracy. I was proud of his strong, healthy teeth, but my mother was ashamed of him in front of the guests. She would hand me a harmonica under the table so I could distract the guests from father's crunching.

"Our daughter," Mother told the guests by way of excuse, "always plays harmonica when we serve chicken."

"Then stop serving chicken on Friday," advised one guest.

"Friday evening without boiled chicken?" another snapped back. "That's supposed to be a Shabbes?"

"It's not the carp or the soup or the chicken that make it a Shabbes!" cried a third.

"What difference does it make if you serve chicken or not?" said a fourth. "The war took everything we had, even our faith. What does Shabbes mean now? It's nothing but a memory. That's all we're celebrating. Let her play her harmonica if she wants."

All eating came to a halt as the argument flared up and then died down, and the guests fixed their eyes on me. I quickly played one song after the other while Father had Erika the maid bring the last bits of chicken from the kitchen. Then he let himself go completely, twisting his head this way and that, savagely attacking the bones as if he were sucking the spirit of his animal forebears. I was terrified he was going to turn into a Neanderthal right then and there, that his clothes might fall off, that fur might start sprouting from his body and big black claws grow out of his fingers. But no, after he'd finished the last bone, he jumped out of his isolation to refill the guests' wineglasses, as elegant and practiced as a waiter, with one hand behind his back.

I WAS A shy, obedient child. Only once did I rebel, when I was twelve years old. One day I refused to go to school. I desperately wanted to talk with Father. I ran after him, shouting, begging: "Talk to me, Papa, please, just once!" He didn't answer. He left the house and didn't come back until after midnight. The next morning I refused to get up, and my parents brought my breakfast to me in bed. Father waved my satchel in my face but I didn't move. They dragged me out of the bed, dressed me, and carried me to the door. I went limp in their arms like a puppet, with no strength in my legs. They put me back in bed and called a doctor who prescribed some medicine, gave me a shot, and bandaged me up—but nothing could get me out of bed. I simply wouldn't move. Three weeks later they hired a private tutor, Fräulein Dübenow, an elderly retired teacher who taught me in bed as though I were an invalid. She brought school to me. Every square inch of my down duvet, which shimmered through its shiny casing, was covered with pencils, rulers, and notebooks. After eight days, when there was no room left for me, I stood up, slipped into my shoes, and started walking with a sure, firm step.

Fräulein Dübenow and I continued to work at the dining table. Before starting she would lay her ancient coin-purse on the table. That was where she kept her watch, and during our lesson I would stare at the purse as if I could read the hands of the watch through the worn leather. When it was time for a break Fräulein Dübenow would ring the bell on the table, and I would run around the room as if it were a schoolyard and eat my snack. Then the lessons would resume. She never checked the time until after we were finished, and she was so accurate that she didn't even need a watch. I resolved that if Fräulein Dübenow ever made a mistake with the time, I would go back to school. But she never did, and so for the rest of my education I was taught at home.

Under Fräulein Dübenow's tutelage I memorized entire dictionaries, archiving each word in my mind, in strict alphabetical order. I bulldozed through entry after entry until finally my head crashed into the hard binding. In twelve months I had memorized a whole twelve-volume children's encyclopedia. Three letters were all I needed and I could picture the entire article, exactly as it looked on the page. I could imitate the sound the paper made as I leafed through the pages. The history of mankind flowed through my brain: I knew kings and cardinals, wars and victories. At my parents' social evenings I would sit on our sofa, boosted by a little silk cushion, and entertain our guests with my inexhaustible knowledge, much to the joy of my parents.

MY MOTHER HAD always been silent, and I had learned to read her intentions in her eyes. One barely perceptible movement would set my course for twenty-four hours, a blink was an admonishing sermon, and from the length of her glance I could draw enough love for an entire day.

She hardly ever spoke, but one time, when she was in bed with a high fever and thought she was going to die, she said: "Forget those two rooms."

That was the only time she mentioned the two rooms where she grew up. After she recovered she wanted to forget everything she'd said.

"If I know that you're thinking about all that, then I can't forget. You have to put everything you heard out of your mind," she told me.

But I didn't want to give up those two rooms; they

were too precious. They were the only place where I felt a breath of freedom, where I could turn somersaults from one corner to the other; I could stamp my feet as much as I wanted; I could light a fire in the oven with old paper and bake golden brown bread for our whole family, for all the uncles and aunts and cousins and . . .

But they were all I had, those two rooms. Even the steps that must have led from the tiny little house out onto the street were unreachably distant for me, like a galactic moon or a star in the boundless expanse of the firmament. In her fever Mother hadn't mentioned any steps.

"I can't, Mama," I said. "I can't forget about those rooms."

"Do it for my sake," she asked, "or else you'll shorten my life."

That was the end of our conversation, and she never said another word about the rooms. A war began raging inside me; I tried to push the images away but they came back, filling my head like a wild, forbidden love. The two rooms seeped into my pores, crept into the deepest recesses of my brain. I wrestled with them, banged my ears, slapped my cheeks, beat my forehead. I was cursed. I would never succeed in freeing my mother from her deep silence. She was right to shut me out. I was ugly and mean.

The only person who actually liked to talk was our maid, Erika, with the wispy blond hair. In the evening she would tell me stories when she put me to bed. Once she told me how her hair got to be so thin: it was just after the end of the war, at her farm in Silesia. The Red Army was celebrating their victory; some soldiers forced their way into the kitchen of their farmhouse, threw her mother, Lore, onto the table, and raped her right in front of her ten-year-old daughter. After they left Erika took a porcelain bowl and held it between her bleeding mother's legs. A few weeks later Erika's beautiful thick hair started falling out in round patches.

Lore and her daughter managed to flee to the west, and later on Erika with the thin hair vowed she would love only Americans. She bore two children to American soldiers and placed them with foster parents so she could earn money working for us. Erika lived boldly and without shame. When my parents were away, she would receive her Americans in my mother's sheer nylon nightgown and disappear with them into my parents' bedroom. After she'd finished her business she would share her presents with me: cheap jewelry, perfume, and candies filled with liqueur. The only thing she kept for herself were the dollar bills, which she rolled up and quickly stashed under the carpet.

Now and then she let me tag along on Sundays, when she took her American children to visit her mother in the Rhön Mountains. Lore was a passionate beekeeper, and with the wire mesh around her head and the leather arm protectors that reached to her elbow she was a fearful sight. Tall, erect, without spots or wrinkles, as if untouched by age, she ruled over her drones and worker bees. She was the true queen. She collected honey but refused to sell it, drank mead out of a silver goblet, and used a stick to chase away all the people who besieged her house wanting to buy some. She stored the honey in small oak barrels that she placed around the entire house; the sweet fragrance was so bewitching that everyone who was passing by stopped at the garden gate as if magically summoned.

Lore put up with her grandchildren only on Sundays. She would comb their wiry hair, cook pancakes, and serve all sorts of dishes with honey. I admired her and longed to be part of the Sunday family. I was even willing to wear Erika's cross around my neck, just to please Grandmother Lore, because one time I overheard her say to her daughter:

"Aren't you ashamed to work for a Jewish family?"

"Just stick to your honeycombs," replied Erika.

"You have to stop working there," her mother continued, "but first you need to bring that poor Jew-child to the right faith."

"That girl is going to keep her own faith. I'm not setting foot anywhere near a church with her. A Russian is a Russian and an American is an American and that's all there is to it," said Erika, and spun around on her heel. And that was the end of the discussion.

When my parents were out of the house, Erika and I played war. Quick as the wind we set up camp in the cellar using mattresses, bedcovers, and thermos bottles that we kept there, hidden from my parents, in case there was a third world war. Erika used charcoal to draw wrinkles on my face and pustules and cracks on my skin. She powdered my hair with dust and ash. I learned to chirp like a bird and hiss like a cat; I slavered and spit, and rubbed myself with rotten onions so that the next time the Russians were drunk with victory they would take me for an ancient, stinking witch.

Erika was my third parent. From her I learned about the world outside the walls of my sheltered existence, about how the Germans survived in their bombed-out cities. Salt and paprika, she explained, have a long shelf life and are good things to keep stocked in the kitchen. They make a good topping for bread during wartime and a little bit goes a long way. To test myself I went for days eating nothing but sandwiches with bread and butter and salt and paprika, clinging to the idea that I would survive all future wars. Everywhere I went I carried a little salt shaker and I hid bags of paprika under my bed. As part of my survival training I ate enormous quantities of paprika and salt without bread, and before long I had weaned myself off of warm meals. That was the beginning of my passion for cold food; I lost weight, and much to the horror of my parents I refused to eat dinner with them and insisted on eating all by myself, at my old scratched-up children's table.

Erika hardly ever cursed and never punished. I always followed her rules. If I crossed the line, she gently corrected me. I could count on her. While she was trimming beans she sang sentimental songs about a young nobleman pining for his love; I hummed along and was so moved that I cried with her.

Erika was close to me in a way my parents were not. I could touch her skin with its ruddy shimmer, put my hand on her heart and feel it pounding. I could imagine how she looked as a newborn, still connected by the umbilical cord to her mother. And in my mind I saw her mother in labor, cursing all men in the world as she pushed, hallucinating the innocent humming of her industrious bees. I imagined Erika cradled in her mother's protective arms, then standing up a year later, holding on to her mother's hand as she took her first clumsy steps. I couldn't ever picture my father as an infant or small child. Our apartment was bare of all memories. There were no yellowed photographs with little children in knitted rompers or stiffly posed people in old-fashioned garb, with dates inked on the back. All the objects that might point to an earlier life had vanished without a trace, as if they'd never existed. For a time I doubted whether Father had even had a childhood and wondered if he hadn't come into the world all grown-up and ready-made with pants and shirt and jacket and tie. Only after I met Mrs. Kugelman did I begin to think that he, too, was once a child. That there was once a woman who took him out of his crib when he cried at night and rocked him in her arms until he calmed down and fell back asleep.

But why wouldn't he speak? What had I done? Why was he punishing me? Father kept me away from his family as if I didn't deserve to know the sacred names of his relatives, as if I were unworthy of learning where he lived or what school he went to or what he ate. If only he'd spoken to me about his memories, then Kalisz would have come to life, a majestic city, a home, a town with mile-long avenues and a river as wide as a lake, far more beautiful and elegant than Mrs. Kugelman's Będzin. I'm sure that Kalisz had its own elite high school, perhaps even funded by someone like Fürstenberg, with a jittery Polish teacher and lazy, rich students. And maybe Father was one of them, a little Adam from Kalisz, a boyish adventurer, a teacher's pet. Or was he more like Kotek? A schoolyard show-off, desperately trying to impress the girls? Why did he change so much after my first day of school? It frightened me. Did it have to do with the war? Did he feel guilty just like Gonna had?

"CAN WE TALK some more about Gonna?" I beg Mrs. Kugelman when she sits down in her armchair the next morning.

"Gonna isn't so important," she says firmly. "He was just one of many: what matters is Będzin."

"Could you at least please tell me something about his family—I'd like to know more."

"You don't know what you're saying. Do you really want to hear how pious girls in Będzin went astray?" she asked mockingly.

"What do you mean? Did pious girls in Będzin go around seducing their schoolmates?"

"How dare you!" she said, highly indignant.

"Then how exactly did they go astray?"

Mrs. Kugelman stares at me for a moment before she answers.

"All right, I'll tell you what I mean." And she settles back into her chair.

12

◄o►

Bluma

"GONNA DIDN'T SEEM TO MIND THAT HIS OWN MOTHER had gone astray. In fact, he was actually proud of her for being so enlightened and progressive.

"Her name was Bluma and she was the oldest daughter of Elizier Silberberg. He had moved to Będzin from Kalisz as a young man—his uncle had died and he took over the family business.

"Elizier Silberberg was a devout Hassid, so he always closed up his shop on Shabbes, at least the front entrance. The back door he kept wide open for emergency sales—he simply couldn't afford to let the workers from the factory next door take their weekly earnings elsewhere to buy liquor. After all, he had to keep his family fed, and they were constantly hungry.

"Here's how it was when it came to religion. Everyone tailored his religion to fit his needs. My own grandparents followed all the traditions, but my father, who had trained as a chemist, considered himself a freethinker and wouldn't even let us light candles on Friday evenings—that's how far he'd moved away from his parents. And Rosenblatt who was the foreman at Father's factory had actually gotten baptized and felt no shame about it. But in Bluma's case it was really her parents who were to blame for her going astray—at least in part. When she was growing up, they saw the enormous changes taking place—telegraphs and radios and telephones and all the other strange new machines—and decided they wanted to give Bluma a little more education than people generally considered proper for daughters from pious homes. So they sent her to a Polish girls' school, thinking that she'd be perfectly safe there and wouldn't fall into the clutches of dangerous men who lie in wait for nice pious girls. Both parents agreed that the religious instruction at the school wasn't anything to worry about: after all, what harm could come from an old bit of brown wood tacked to the wall with Jesus hanging on it?

"Her parents expected that Bluma would keep on being a nice pious girl, that her schooling might raise her head just enough so she could see out a little farther—but they didn't want her to see *too* much, and of course they fully expected the rest of her body to stay exactly where it was—in other words, nice and pious. But each of us has a head of our own, and we don't always follow our parents' wishes.

"Bluma worked hard at her studies and paid attention in class. She also listened carefully to what the Polish girls were saying in the schoolyard. As time went on she sensed a new feeling growing inside her, something she called a joy for life. She first felt it while writing—it made her happy to find a thought and jot it down and give it a voice. And little by little, as if she were awakening from a deep sleep, her whole view of life began to change. During recess she started putting a little soap on her bangs so they would curl up a bit—you could barely see it, though. Then she'd straighten them back out on her way home, at least at first. She started tying her skirts a little tighter and rolling her sleeves a little higher, naturally only on account of the summer heat. But then she kept them rolled up all through the winter as well. Her joy of life grew stronger and stronger, filling her head with new ideas, and her body was so pliant, it easily followed along. By the end of her schooling Bluma had moved so far from her faith, she didn't want to go back—it felt cozy but confined. She passed her graduation exams and was about to enter the university, but her parents rescued her just in time. What would happen to her if she became even more freethinking, so that pretty soon there'd be no controlling her, and what young man would choose a girl like that?

"Gonna's grandparents didn't have those kind of worries because for boys there was an ancient system of schooling already in place. Everything was laid out for them, since they were considered guardians of tradition. First they went to the cheder and later they moved on to the yeshiva. There they were only among boys, so their bodies were undistracted and their minds were free to focus on the texts of the great masters.

"Gonna's father, Pinye, had a twin brother named Mendel who was known as 'Mendel with the black spot' because he had a dark birthmark on his right cheek. Both boys were eager students. In fact Pinye might have devoted his whole life to holy scripture if love hadn't treated him so badly. Every day when the brothers left the yeshiva to go home, Pinye would look up at a window across the street, and every day the same beautiful girl would be looking back at him with her beautiful green eyes. You've never seen a green like that, which stood out all the more because her eyebrows were so dark and full. Her neck was slender, her face a perfect, tender oval. Maite—that was her name—would linger at the window for just a moment, and that tiny instant of bliss was enough for Pinye to think of eternity.

"But Pinye wanted more than a tiny instant: he wanted to look at Maite any time and all the time. His parents were overjoyed at the idea, but Maite's parents were not so enthusiastic. They had doubts about their prospective son-in-law's scholarliness. Pinye hadn't yet drawn enough wisdom from the font of ancient knowledge, hadn't studied hard enough to merit their extremely beautiful daughter. Day after day Maite waited for him in the window, showing her round, golden-green eyes, and she kept leading him on like that until one day she was finally married off to a learned Hassid from Katowice, who was much more to her parents' liking than Gonna's father.

"The day after the wedding, as Pinye was leaving the yeshiva, Mendel with the black spot tried to hurry his brother home, but Pinye tore himself loose, stopped, and took one final look at the window, hoping to catch a last glimpse of the beautiful Maite, or at least see her shadow or at the very least discover some small sign, a flower, a little twig, or even an empty glass—anything would have sufficed as a token of farewell.

"But instead of that he found Maite's younger sister, Pepa, waiting at the windowsill, watching for Gonna's father just like Maite had. She was very pretty, too, and her eyes were grayish-green. But Pinye had had enough. Maite's family is making fun of me, he thought: these rude, uncouth people are setting out the younger sister to trap me, and if I wind up liking her they'll marry her off to someone else, and then they'll set out an even younger sister, and they won't stop until they've run out of daughters.

"All these love troubles made it hard for him to stay focused on the holy scripture. Suddenly the letters seemed jinxed; they started running together when he read. What was the point of being so devout when people who were supposedly pious treated him so shabbily? He wasn't the same anymore, and he didn't know what he was going to do with himself.

"By the time he met Bluma a year later, he had no trouble deciding on her. Her parents, Velvel and Chana Baile, had suggested the match, thinking that Pinye might like a free-thinking woman—and besides, better a freethinker than no wife at all. And as it turned out, Pinye did like Bluma, and while there was no feeling of eternity this time, he very much appreciated her clear brown eyes with their firm strong gaze. Their wedding finally put an end to all the irksome business about love, and never again would he be affected by the color of a woman's eyes, no matter how extraordinary.

"Bluma was full of energy and quickly showed who wore the pants in the family, ruling over her husband and their four children. She made up her mind that their household would be a freethinking one, and little by little she cast off the old customs. They even ate fresh Christian ham in their home, but only in the kitchen and only off butcher paper, since Bluma was very careful that the plates stayed undefiled for her parents. Out of love for them she kept her pantry strictly divided into separate sections for dairy and meat. Each cupboard had its own dishes, pots, pans, cooking spoons, and dish towels stacked on wooden shelves. Beneath the dishes for meat was a broad, velvet-lined double drawer full of precious Shabbes silver: beautiful sterling knives and forks, and separate services with shimmering yellow handles for fish and meat, coffee and dessert. Her parents insisted on carefully inspecting everything before sitting down at their daughter's table. And her husband's parents wouldn't even do that—they worried that the dietary laws weren't being kept and refused to eat a single bite. They wouldn't even touch the glasses. All they would accept was water, which they drank out of silver cups they brought themselves."

"IF THEY'D BEEN my parents-in-law, I wouldn't have allowed them in my house!"

"That's easy to say," said Mrs. Kugelman. "But Chana

Baile and Velvel were strict Hassids, and Bluma was trying to honor their beliefs. You should have seen the holiday meals at their house! Chana Baile would take her finest tablecloth and set the table with silver cups and candelabras and fresh loaves of challah that smelled so delicious underneath the embroidered cloths. And then the whole family would sit down together—thirty or forty people all at the same table."

Thirty or forty people! I can't imagine a group like that. My parents' guests were all the relatives I had: uncles and aunts for just an evening. An artificial family with members that changed daily.

"Were there a lot of Hassidic Jews in Będzin? I thought it was a modern town."

"It was. We had industrial firms, banks, and businesses," Mrs. Kugelman said proudly. "But there were also a lot of very devout Jews. In fact, they even had a special name for Będzin—the Jerusalem of Zagłębie."

"Jerusalem of Zagłębie." I tried saying the phrase. A wonderfully beautiful name that melted on my tongue like chocolate. Did the Hassidim in Kalisz have such a sonorous name for their part of town? Golden Jerusalem, perhaps? Was my father born in Golden Jerusalem? He came from a devout family; I'd heard him talk about it at the table. But Father had cast all the customs aside and he even railed against religion although never against those who practiced it—so all I was able to learn from him was a fundamental respect for the piety of others.

I know it's no use asking Mrs. Kugelman about Kalisz. It would probably just irritate her.

"A beautiful name," is all I say.

"Not to everyone. At our school we made fun of the Hassidic children. Adam in particular used to split his sides laughing at their old-fashioned dress, their hairstyle, their Stone Age lifestyle."

"Why so malicious?"

"We all thought of ourselves as progressive. Especially Gonna. He didn't want to be associated with his Hassidic relatives—Mendel and Rivka Sheina and their children. He never visited his cousins except after dark, just so we wouldn't see. And Adam wouldn't even set foot in the rynek—the old market square where a lot of the pious Jews lived. But I went there every Thursday afternoon to help Mrs. Żmigród deliver her cake to her sister's family. Mrs. Żmigród couldn't manage because of her gouty hands, so I carried it for her," says Mrs. Kugelman.

13

◄○►

Hassidic poker

"NOW BEFORE WE GET INTO ANYTHING ELSE, LET ME TELL
you about that cake. You should have seen the way it
puffed up, and the crust was perfect, with just the right
amount of crunch, and the filling was so light it was like
eating air. That's because Mrs. Żmigród always used the
finest ingredients. She baked it on Thursday morning, after
I'd left for school, and once she finished baking she would
get dressed up for the visit. First she'd brush out her gray
hair and give it a little wave, and then she'd pile it into a
bun. After that she'd change into her fancy black-and-
white polka-dot dress, which I always thought looked a
little too tight around her hips. By the time I came back
from school she'd be all ready to go and we'd take the cake
to her sister Rivka Sheina, but it was really meant for the
children: Mirele, Yossel, and the other brothers and sisters,
all of whom were on the plump side, no doubt thanks to
our weekly visits. The reason Mrs. Żmigród did her baking

in the morning while I was still at school was to keep me from giving away any secrets to Rivka Sheina, who never failed to ask me for the recipe.

"Mendel and Rivka Sheina and their family lived right next to the prayer room of the Krimilow Hassidim, so at dawn they woke up to the sound of praying and after sunset they went to bed to the same quiet singsong—in fact, the children couldn't imagine falling asleep any other way.

"Gonna's cousin Mirele was as devout as the rest of her family. Every morning she walked to school with her two friends. And every morning when they reached the nonkosher butcher shop on Małachowski Street, they'd make a wide detour, holding their noses until they were well past the entrance, because they didn't want to smell the unkosher meat. Mirele would squeeze her nose so tight, it turned white. The girls didn't dare breathe until they'd reached the next street corner, when they could inhale some good, pure air. Then Mirele's nose would quickly get its rosy color back. On their way home from school they'd do the same thing. I'm sure Mirele's nose was so well trained it would close up all by itself as soon as it came near anything unkosher.

"On Friday afternoons Mirele and her friends used to go up and down the neighborhood carrying a big basket. They'd stop outside each building and call out at the top of their voices: 'Lekhem.' The word worked like a charm. Windows would fly open and golden sweet challah loaves and poppy braids that had been baked especially for the collection would come raining down. For a moment Będzin looked like some fabled land of milk and honey. Every now and then the girls had a hard time catching the challah, especially if it had been flung down from one of the upper stories. To make sure none of the donations wound up on the pavement, Mirele's two friends would spread out their long skirts. It was Mirele's job to go inside and receive cakes or anything else that had to be carried downstairs, which she tucked away in the basket. Sometimes, when the fun was at a peak, Mirele would join her friends, catching the challah with her basket and using her hand to cushion the landing. Of course some apartments were stingier than others, and the friends would have to hold their basket underneath a single window. Mirele was a little clumsy, so she occasionally missed a loaf or lost her footing, but most of the challah survived intact. Eventually the three girls would make their rounds to the poorest people in town, quietly leaving the gifts outside their door, so that on Fridays they, too, could eat their fill of the sweet braided bread.

"Despite her good behavior, Mendel with the black spot wasn't always so pleased with his daughter Mirele. He wagged his finger at her and complained that she walked too fast, talked too much, and stuck her nose into places where a well-behaved daughter shouldn't. And it was true, too: Mirele found out things no one was supposed to know, things she sometimes told me in secret. For instance, the fact that on Christmas day the Hassidic Jews went to the shtibl the way they always did, but instead of praying, they played cards—something completely unheard of—and they weren't pretending, either, they played for money, with real winning and real losing. And the reason they did this was to thwart that other God, whose power on that day was particularly strong, what with all the Christians praying so fervently. The Christian God might start feeling overconfident and take what wasn't meant for him. The Hassidim didn't want to risk having any of their own prayers wind up in the wrong hands, and so instead of praying at all, the pious Jews played cards. Mirele told me about their trick but made me promise not to tell another soul."

HASSIDIC JEWS PLAYING poker on Christmas—what will she come up with next? I better watch out or I'll become completely addicted to her stories. I know I have to put a stop to this, but I can't help myself. "Mrs. Kugelman," I blurt out, "I'm going to book a double room and from now on you can just sleep here."

She doesn't seem at all surprised by my suggestion and immediately accepts my invitation. She gets up and goes to the bathroom without a word and without first asking my permission. But that's all right: tonight I'll let her use my towel and soap, I'll wash her back, I'll even share my tooth-brush with her.

I race downstairs and explain to the surly clerk in the lobby that I'd like to have a large, comfortable double room right away, and for the rest of my stay.

"Why, is your boyfriend coming?" he asks, not even trying to hide his curiosity.

"No, it's for Mrs. Kugelman."

"I can give you one for three nights, but that's all I have."

"What do you mean?" I protest. "The hotel is half empty." I wonder if all the hotels in Tel Aviv have conspired against me.

"I'm afraid I can't guarantee anything more than that," he says.

"I don't need a guarantee. What I need is a room," I say. I have a hunch that Koby may have told the man about the incident in the freezer—they're on good terms because he sends fares to Koby in exchange for a small commission. In any event, I'm convinced that the hotel staff is now trying to get rid of me.

"I can let you have a double room for three nights," the man repeats.

"That's the first I've ever heard of a hotel not wanting to fill empty rooms. I'd like to speak to the manager," I say boldly.

"Those are my instructions," he whispers. "It's on account of Mrs. Kugelman." Then he warns me against her. The hotel would have shooed her out long ago, but Mrs. Kugelman is a friend of the owner, who comes from a neighboring town in Poland. That's the only reason she's allowed to sit in the lobby. They have an agreement that Mrs. Kugelman can speak to no more than four guests a year, and then only during the off-season.

"Why just four?" I ask.

It turns out the owner is worried about the hotel's reputation. And that Mrs. Kugelman doesn't keep her end of the bargain. Apparently I'm the seventh guest this year.

"The fifth was a young man from Switzerland," says the clerk. "He was here only three weeks ago. After Mrs. Kugelman made a few visits he refused to leave his room. His parents—survivors from Poland—had to fly him back to Zurich. Just this morning I was asking about his health."

I pay a little extra for the largest double room, which has an oversized, heart-shaped bed. It's the honeymoon suite, richly furnished with white panels and red, satiny linens. From this moment on Mrs. Kugelman and I are joined together like a newly married couple. She will sit in one of the comfortable armchairs and I will lie awake in our newlywed bed, listening to her stories of Będzin.

BEHIND OUR CLOSED curtains the hours just slip by. We don't even notice the cool morning breeze that blows in just before sunrise. Koby supplies Mrs. Kugelman with warm meals from the restaurant, and me with ice cream from a stand on the beach. Every day at the exact same time he pushes through our door, bringing a blast of fresh air and a burst of bright Mediterranean daylight. It's obvious he wants to tear open the curtains, let in the noises from the street, the stench, the moist air. What he wants most of all is to scare off all the brooding thoughts, drive away the old stories, lure us onto the beach and into the dazzling midday sun.

Koby puts down the tray, sets our table, and invites us to eat. I sense that he's watching me closely, undoubtedly checking to see if I am displaying the same symptoms as the man from Switzerland.

"So how long do you expect this to go on?" he asks me in quiet reproach.

"Until I've heard all there is to hear," I answer curtly.

I ask Mrs. Kugelman to keep talking even as we eat. I don't touch my ice cream; all I do is hold the cold cup gently in my fingers and let her feed me with stories from her town. Like an infant I suck in the warm milk of her words, I begin to thrive, I grow up all over again in the space of a few hours. I feel as though a tree were growing inside me, its leaves flooded with sunlight. Roots meld with my legs, branches stretch out from my shoulders, flowers blossom on my arms and sprout from my fingertips.

Grateful, I plunge into the golden bath of Mrs. Kugelman's memories. Together we gild the roofs of her town, pave the streets with white marble, construct a crystal dome over Będzin. I envy her for the images that fill her head. I want to breathe the same air she does, eat what she puts in her mouth, copy the pattern of her speech, and sample her favorite dishes, picking out the most delicious morsels just for the two of us. Under Mrs. Kugelman's spell I regain my taste for warm food: hot, crispy brown and pan-seared dishes. I even start to enjoy little innocent fishes, heavily spiced and stuck on a stick and grilled. Carefully probing with my tongue, then chewing more and more strongly, I shove everything that is edible into my mouth. I ask Koby to bring me a second serving, and when I've finished that, I start digging away at Mrs. Kugelman's meal. Without a word she passes me all her plates.

While I am flourishing like a young eucalyptus tree, Mrs. Kugelman shrinks and withers; her skin turns yellow and transparent like old brittle parchment. Her pauses grow longer, her throat runs dry, her voice begins to falter. On the third day she feels uneasy and wants to go home to rest for the afternoon, but I block the door. I can't allow her to go. I hold her back, refuse to let her out of the room, my resolve strengthened by the passion her stories have awakened.

"Mrs. Kugelman, stay and tell me all you can about Będzin!"

She obeys my command and sits back down, too tired to speak. At the end of the third day Koby brings us our supper and looks at Mrs. Kugelman with concern.

But it's our last night in the room, and I want to make it a celebration. I take out my aunt's silver chest. I light one of the hotel candles, polish the tarnished silverware, and dust the handles. Visibly weakened, Mrs. Kugelman takes a seat at the table, tormenting herself with every bite. All of a sudden she stops and picks up a fish knife. She holds it at arm's length and, straining her eyes, stares at the engraved design. She gives a start.

"How did this get here?"

"Why, have you seen it before?" I ask.

"Where did you get this?"

With a hint of pride I answer, "I inherited it from my aunt Halina."

"Your aunt was named Halina?"

"Yes."

"This was the fish service that Gonna carried to Palestine. I was there when his mother packed it in his suitcase."

"This same service? Are you sure?"

"Of course I'm sure," says Mrs. Kugelman. "I remember the mother-of-pearl handles with the engraved fish."

"Why would she send a fish service from Poland to Palestine?"

"It was meant to be a gesture of goodwill. Bluma was trying to reconcile with her daughter. She hadn't written Halina a single word in two whole years."

"Why?"

"Because Halina had run away. She eloped with Dolek in 1937 and they emigrated to Palestine. Halina was seventeen at the time, still half a child, she hadn't even finished school. Bluma was very angry with her. Didn't you know that?"

"How should I know that? But why send a fish service? Surely a young couple in Palestine had more use for other things than a few fish forks."

"Bluma had been given this service as a wedding present. It was an heirloom, very valuable. Nothing was more natural than to pass it on to her eldest daughter. Incidentally, the fish service was only the first installment; the rest of the silverware was supposed to follow. But then nothing else ever arrived. You didn't hear anything about that?"

"No, I've never heard of anybody named Bluma. Or Gonna, for that matter."

"And Simon? Are you familiar with the name Simon?" Mrs. Kugelman drills away with her question.

"No, there was no Simon either."

"You must have heard of Simon. Simon, the boy we called Gonna, is Halina's brother! Are you sure Halina really is your aunt?"

"Yes, of course," I say, annoyed. "She's my father's sister."

"So if Halina is your aunt, then you have to be related to Gonna. You might even be his daughter . . ."

"Me? Gonna's daughter? I couldn't be. My father came from Kalisz, not Będzin."

"What was his name?"

"My father's name was Max Silberberg and was called Meir. Not Gonna."

"Wait a moment," she says slowly, drawing out the words. "Meir, yes, Meir Elizier Silberberg. That's the name that was written in large letters above the grocery store next to the factory. I remember exactly. I passed by that store all the time. Gonna must have taken his mother's father's name when he went back to Europe."

I think about all the fish forks in the world. Every restaurant of any standing has them. Chased, chromed, silver-plated, gold-plated fish services. Every fifth family in Israel uses one to set the Friday night table for the traditional meal. Surely I can't have a brand-new father from Będzin named Gonna just on account of a fish service.

Mrs. Kugelman guesses my thoughts. "You know," she says, "lots of people changed their names after the war. Nothing from earlier seemed right anymore. Some had

protected themselves with papers that belonged to someone else and kept the name that had saved them. Others
took the name of their wife, so they could start over fresh
but honor a memory. And some changed their date of birth,
making themselves younger by five years, to compensate
for the years that were stolen."

"Did any of this work?" I ask, skeptical.

"Not really. But it did bring them a little relief. They no
longer felt quite so helpless, quite so much at the mercy of
fate."

"Did this Gonna change his birth place, too?"

"It certainly sounds that way. You said your father came
from Kalisz. That's where Gonna's grandfather Elizier
came from, so it would have been a logical place for him to
pick. He did have roots there, and by choosing Kalisz he
could try to put Będzin behind him."

"But why would he want to do that? Będzin was such a
wonderful place. Why not treasure the memory?"

"When Adam, the Polish girl, and I arrived in Haifa in
1948 on the refugee ship, Gonna was standing at the dock
to meet us. When we told him Kotek hadn't survived, he
broke down. We had to hold him up. We spent that first
night with Gonna at Halina's. It was Friday evening. We
had our first meal in the land we had only dreamed about.
Halina served a white fish from the Mediterranean and
we ate it with the silver service from our lost Polish town.
She gave each of us a fork to commemorate the evening.
We were so thankful. That was our first present after all
those terrible years, and we saw it as a good omen. The

next morning Gonna disappeared. He didn't even say good-
bye. He sailed back to Europe on the empty refugee ship."

"Did he ever return?"

"No, that was the last we heard of him."

"Did you ever try to get in touch with him?"

"No, Gonna had changed. He tormented himself with
the thought that he had abandoned his family. He survived
in Palestine, while his whole family was sent to their death.
Back then no one who survived could be counted as happy."

I CAN'T BEAR it any longer and jump out of my chair.

"Mrs. Kugelman, you better leave right this minute," I
tell her. Then I fling open the door and practically push
her out of the room.

My heart pounding, I quickly open the silver chest and
count. Out of twelve settings, three fish knives and four
forks are missing. But even if Halina did give away four
forks, does that prove that I am Gonna's daughter? Couldn't
I be the daughter of someone else, some lucky person who
just happens to possess the missing pieces from Halina's
silver chest? But I don't want a different father. I'm used to
my silent father. How could my father possibly be the
same person as Gonna? Ridiculous. Father had nothing in
common with Gonna. Father was a sober businessman
focused on profit margins and bottom lines, while Gonna
was a passionate student interested in literature and philosophy. Gonna was sharp and clever, while Father was a
little ponderous; he wavered a long time before making
a decision. Gonna always had a book in hand and was the

fastest reader in Będzin; I never saw Father pick up a book, and it took him hours just to read the paper. There's no way a person could change that much! On the other hand, Gonna did have a sister named Halina, just like my father, and she owned a fish service with the exact same engraving I have right here. On top of that, he was the grandson of a Silberberg who came from Kalisz. Was it all mere coincidence? What if Father had assumed the name of his mother's father? Does that mean I grew up in a house of lies built by a man who had slipped into the skin of another? Who am I? What's my real name? Should I take the name that Father discarded and reject the one I grew up with? Are my parents even really my parents? I feel like a stranger to myself; I hardly recognize myself anymore. A lump forms in my throat; I feel like I'm going to suffocate. I'll stop breathing and the first parts to die will be my hands and legs and then the rest of me will follow. I have to control the panic that's coming. I need ice, a lot of ice. I ring up Daud in the kitchen, but he doesn't answer.

Gasping for air, I jam my head into the tiny refrigerator and lick the frost off the miniature bottles. That calms me down just enough so I can think. If Gonna were my father, then surely one of all the guests who passed through my parents' house would have recognized him and called him by his real name. Or was there some kind of unspoken agreement among the survivors, among all those who had lost their loved ones? Theirs was a twilight world from which we who were born after were excluded.

But if I hadn't been born after . . . if I'd been born back

then in Poland, there wouldn't have been room enough for any friends at my wedding, because the hall would have been packed with all my relatives. In the end, though, I came into the world with a nakedness for which there is no clothing; I belong to a club with an invisible membership that's scattered across the globe—the club of children who grow up without a past.

The freedom to live an independent life was not given to me in the cradle. My father and the man who was hiding behind him conceived me in a moment of crazy hope, in the belief that the power of my birth might let them wrest a new life out of all the death. The infant in the stroller that was shown off with such pride was meant to replace the entire lost family: father, mother, sisters, and brothers. The tiny human bundle that was me was supposed to mend the torn chain of the generations. But I shattered all my parents' hopes, because at least up to now I am single and childless. The end of the chain.

The ice in the freezer is sharp; the cold stings my cheeks and revives my head. My mouth moves; sounds arise in my throat and on my tongue. Sentences take shape from the words that are stacked on top of one another in the dusty chambers of my mind, where they've been stored for decades, shut off from the world, waiting to be used—words that now peel off my lips, trembling as they come to life. If Gonna is your father, I hear myself saying, then Bluma is your grandmother, Pinye is your grandfather, and Mendel with the black spot is your great-uncle. Keep repeating it until you believe it: Gonna's family belongs to me. His grandfather

Elizier who sold liquor is my great-grandfather. The people of Będzin are mine. Kołłątaj Street and Małachowski Street are mine as well. I say these things, and I feel a rising joy; the whole room is dancing, dancing with all my relatives who had disappeared. I can't believe how many there are. They have come back and I have found them.

I am bursting with curiosity; I want to know all I can about my family, what they looked like, how they dressed, how they lived. I accept Gonna as my new father. And in return he gives me a priceless gift—an entire town. Even the remotest possibility of paternity is enough for me—even one tenth of a thousandth percent chance. Gonna *is* my new father.

THE NIGHT PASSES, and in the morning Mrs. Kugelman comes back, looking much recovered. I've been working on a family tree that lists all my new relatives and quickly stash the paper out of sight.

"I'm sorry for acting the way I did yesterday," I say, ashamed.

"What matters is Będzin."

"You're right."

Mrs. Kugelman stares at the table as though searching for something. But I've hidden the chest beneath the bed, just to be on the safe side. Today I'd rather put Gonna aside. Instead I want to hear all about my new relatives, about Mirele and Mendel with the black spot and Rivka Sheina and all the cousins.

"Back then, in Poland . . . did Rivka Sheina or Mirele dream of coming here? Did they ever think that they would one day swim on the seashore of the Holy Land?"

"They wouldn't have been surprised in the least," she answers with a gentle smile.

"Why not?"

"Because the Hassidim have always had their share of miracles."

"What kind of miracles?"

14

◄o►

Wonders never cease

"VERY REAL MIRACLES! IN THE HASSIDIC NEIGHBORHOOD by the rynek, where Mirele and her family lived, miracles were practically an everyday occurrence. But wherever you have miracles you also have a lot of arguing, since what one group sees as miraculous another group sees as questionable. And in Będzin we had more groups than you could count, and each one had its own dynasty of leaders, and each thought their rebbe was the most wondrous of all. There were the Gerers and the Sochaczewers, the Radomskers and the Pinczowers, the Aleksandrers and the Krimilowers, and who knows how many others.

"The Krimilowers believed that their rebbe was leading them closest to the highest truth, while the Radomskers were convinced they were the most devout. Both the Gerers and the Radomskers looked down on the Pinczowers as less learned, and no one revered their rebbe more than the Aleksandrer Hassidim.

"Mirele's grandfather Velvel, who belonged to the Alek-sandrer group, was a devout Hassid and a very modest man. He made sure his soft dark beard didn't attract attention and wore his black caftan in his own quiet way. Every morn-ing he tucked his peyes behind his ears just so he wouldn't stand out in any way. He walked through the streets taking small steps, scarcely touching the ground. But he was always a welcome guest at *simches*, when he would let himself go, leaving all modesty behind, and join the circle of men, sing-ing and dancing and stamping with his feet—enraptured, wild, exuberant.

"Once when Velvel was young he traveled to Zgierz to seek some business advice—that's what people used to do—from the great Yitzchok Menachem himself, the Grand Rabbi of all the Aleksandrer Hassidim. When he got there he took his place in the long line of pious Jews waiting to see the rebbe. But he was so nervous that when his turn came, he gave up his place and went back to the end of the line because he needed a little more time to think through his questions. One and a half days later he was ready. He stepped humbly up to the rebbe and asked his blessing for a small candy factory he planned to construct in his home-town of Wolbrom, at the fairgrounds, where all the children came to play. His brother-in-law had given him a special recipe that could transform little pieces of sugar into candy. As soon as the business started to pay off, Velvel intended to expand and hire two apprentices.

"But the rebbe advised against opening a factory in Wolbrom and recommended a place ten kilometers away, a tiny village with just a handful of houses. Velvel stared at the rabbi in amazement and asked him who would buy candy in such a small place, but the rabbi remained adamant and refused to give his blessing for a factory in Wolbrom.

"All the way home Velvel thought long and hard: on the one hand, he didn't want to build his factory in Wolbrom against the advice of the rebbe, but neither did he feel confident enough to set up a factory several kilometers away, in a tiny village with a single street. So for the time being he went on selling stockings and sundries, and lived comfortably off what he brought in. One year later, when his twin sons Pinye and Mendel were sixteen, the First World War broke out, and the Cossacks attacked Wolbrom. Velvel, his wife, Chana Baile, and their two sons managed to escape just in time, carrying only the most necessary things. On the way out of town they saw that the Cossacks had started a huge fire right on the spot where Velvel had wanted to build his factory. The fairgrounds and the surrounding houses all burned down, so that nothing remained except ash and carbonized pieces of wood. As they were fleeing, Velvel and his family passed through the tiny village the rebbe had picked with his seventh sense. By a miracle, all the buildings had been spared—the Cossack horses had churned up huge clouds of dust that kept the little village completely hidden and safe from harm for two whole days."

"CHANA BAILE AND Velvel loved telling stories about their miraculous rabbi. But neither of their two sons stayed with the Aleksandrers. First Pinye married the freethinking

Bluma and under her influence abandoned his parents' devout ways. And scarcely had Velvel come to terms with the loss of one son than Mendel began to question the wisdom of Rabbi Yitzchok Menachem. He set out to find someone even more knowledgeable, someone who would be able to answer any question on any topic he could think of. Mendel traveled for a long time and saw, heard, and experienced many things. In one town he met a rabbi who refused to keep any money in his house overnight because it was too base a thing. His followers provided for him generously, but the rebbe only kept what was needed to maintain his court and doled out the rest among his people. And if there was any left after that he would open his window and fling it outside, so that the coins flew out onto the street and the paper money fluttered into town, where it settled, guided by God, in front of the poorest houses.

"Another rabbi had a very different attitude toward wealth. He had inherited a glass factory through his marriage to a rich heiress, and the enterprise was very profitable. The rabbi took over the business, taught several of his followers modern accounting skills, and increased the prosperity of all.

"Everywhere he went, Mendel met fathers who had left their families to pray at the court of a revered rabbi. Many were very poor men who felt overwhelmed at home and were unable to provide for their families. Some stayed for a year and others stayed forever.

"Mendel felt sad that he couldn't decide which rabbi was the wisest, and in the end he returned to his parents.

A little later on he married the seamstress Rivka Sheina, and soon they were expecting Mirele, their first child. The young couple moved into a small apartment right next to the Krimilowers' shtibl. And that's where the miracle happened. Mendel with the black spot found his happiness. He didn't need to travel across the world because the rabbi he could believe in was right next door. The Krimilower Rebbe always pondered a matter a long time before giving advice and pronouncing his blessing. He was able to rid Mendel of all the doubts that were plaguing him, and answer all his questions about life as well as death."

"ONCE WHEN MIRELE was little, her family suffered a terrible misfortune. Her brother Shloime, who was younger by nine months, contracted diphtheria, and just when everyone thought he'd recovered, and Rivka Sheina had gone back to helping Mendel in the shop, the little boy suddenly stopped breathing. Mirele was desperate and called on Grandfather Velvel to look after the boy while she ran to fetch her parents. But by the time they got there Grandfather Velvel was nowhere to be found: he'd gone straight to his shtibl to ask the Aleksandrer Rebbe for advice, and there he was told that the rebbe had peered into the vast heaven and seen Shloime in a beautiful garment with freshly combed hair, as sweet as could be, with no sign of illness, playing among the angels, in a place from which no one returns. The rabbi told Velvel to go home and to console the parents with the knowledge that within a year they would bring a son to life. They should name him Yosef, after the rebbe, and the boy would later become just as learned a scholar as his namesake."

"AND DID RIVKA Sheina have a second son?" I ask.

"Yossel was born nine months after the rabbi made his prediction."

"And did he really become a rabbi?"

"No, that's where the miracle of the Aleksandrers came to an end," says Mrs. Kugelman, laughing. "Although that boy really was very gifted, and I'm sure he could have become a rabbi if he'd had a mind to. But he was determined to go to our school with all the freethinkers. Mendel was furious, and Velvel was so grief-stricken that Mendel was worried about the old man's weak heart.

"'Your disobedience is going to bring your grandfather to an early grave,' he yelled at Yossel.

"But the boy wouldn't budge, and that was that."

15

◄o►

Yossel

"Even as a child," says Mrs. Kugelman, "Yossel had the face of an adult. He looked as though he'd skipped childhood and went straight to being a strapping young man. Long before his bar mitzvah he had dark shadows on his upper lip and cheeks. His brothers and sisters were all pretty plump but he was all muscle.

"Yossel's parents sent him to their rebbe's shul, where he studied sacred texts in the morning and other subjects in the afternoon. And the more he studied, the more he wanted to learn. He yearned to go to a school like ours, so he could have a profession for later life and not wind up poor. He mentioned his plans to one of his teachers—a man by the name of Langfuss, who taught Polish at the shul, and Langfuss promised to help. He knew of two other boys named Nussan and Ari who had similar ideas, and Langfuss managed to get the Fürstenberg Gymnasium to take all three boys without tuition. In fact, the school even offered to pay for their books and uniforms. Langfuss called his protégés together and told them the good news: Nothing more stood in the way of their attending the Fürstenberg Gymnasium, he proclaimed solemnly; all that was left was for their fathers to sign the application.

"Yossel was overjoyed. As he walked home from the shul that afternoon, he was already picturing himself in his new school uniform, imagining the life he would lead there in the middle of the rynek, poring over his books under the eyes of the pious. But instead of the signature they were hoping for, all each boy got from his father was a beating, and Yossel got the worst. Mendel was outraged that his son would consider going to a school as freethinking as ours, where boys didn't even have to keep their heads covered. He was so mad, he tore an armrest off an old wobbly chair and started beating Yossel so hard that the boy fled out to the street. Mendel chased after him, brandishing the arm-rest, and the two of them raced like that through the streets of Będzin until Yossel was so desperate, he dashed into the Christian cemetery. That was one place he knew he'd be safe from his father because a Hassid would never set foot inside a Christian cemetery, no matter what the danger.

"After that they didn't speak for months. And during this time Yossel decided to commit a violent act and cut off his peyes. He dreamed of wearing nothing but a small yar-mulke, like the more modern-looking boys. He was sure that his father would be horrified to see his bare cheeks, but as long as they were arguing, Yossel didn't feel any need to justify himself.

"Still, he had no idea how he should go about it, whether he should trim off a little bit each day, until all that was left of his beautiful peyes were two short stumps, or whether he should save his money and go to Lachman the barber so he could cut them off with a single stroke. Yossel paced back and forth in front of Lachman's shop, brooding. The barber saw those paces and knew what they meant. He'd seen a lot of men walk up and down in front of his shop, tormented by doubt. Some had no choice: if you were a father trying to keep your family fed, you had to do business in the cities, and that meant making sure your hair was cut and your beard was trimmed. Otherwise people wouldn't buy what you were selling. And once you stepped into that barbershop there was no going back: the new look demanded new clothes, and the men would go straight from Lachman's to the tailor next door. There they'd set aside their long black coat, full of shame, and buy a short overcoat for the journey, which was easy to travel in and do business."

"YOSSEL SHUDDERED AT the thought of losing his peyes—it was more than a haircut, it was an amputation, and once removed, his side curls would never grow back so beautifully and innocently. Everyone would see right away that he was a traitor. Lachman had a special knife for cutting peyes, with a white heft that sat well in the hand, because most of the victims shrank back at the last moment. The blade was particularly sharp because both locks had to be cut off in one motion, so fast the sinner couldn't see it in the mirror, assuming he was even capable of watching in the first place. After the fatal moment Lachman would step back elegantly, leaving his client for a moment of reflection. Then he would take his large shears in his skilled hands and very gently start working on the pitiful stumps and the main head of hair, transforming them into a modern hair-style, with brilliantine and scented hair-water.

"After the procedure Yossel ran home to get the expected beating over with as quickly as possible. At first Mendel was taken aback when he saw the strange boy with the familiar face, but once he recognized his own son, he was filled with horror and fell into a deep, merciful unconsciousness. For Yossel that was the worst punishment of all, but even so, he never let his peyes grow back out."

MRS. KUGELMAN SENSES that it's time to stop, since I need to pack my things, and heads for the door. Our honeymoon is over; I have to move to another room. They've already turned off the air-conditioning, and the heat pushes in through the cracks of the honeymoon suite. Stripped down to my underwear, I sweat as I finish packing. Then I shove my luggage next to the door, throw on some clothes, and take the elevator down to the reception desk.

The clerk and I soon come to an agreement. I promise not to cause any trouble with Mrs. Kugelman and he gives me a nice room on the floor for preferred business guests, which has open access to a small lounge, where the stale soft drinks and dried-out cookies are free for the taking.

*   *   *

When Mrs. Kugelman settles in an armchair the next morning, I ask her if Halina had also given her a fish knife at some later time.

"I never laid eyes on Halina after the day I arrived," she answers.

"Never?"

"Never. So there's a knife missing as well?"

"Three of them."

"Back then in Poland it was complete."

"Really?"

"Yes, really. But what difference does it make?"

"I just want to know."

"And if you find out, then will you be happy?"

"I want to know as much as I can."

"For some things there is no answer. We have to live with not knowing," she says, shaking her head.

"Look," she says to console me when she notices the disappointment in my face, "the fish knives aren't so important. People only ate carp on Shabbes, and only the rich people had a fish service. The important thing was having enough food for Shabbes in the first place," she said, quietly. Then she breaks off the conversation, stops paying attention to me, sets her feet comfortably on her bag, fixes her hair, and gives a little smile.

16

<o>

The cholent baker

"ONE THURSDAY—THAT WAS OUR MARKET DAY,
remember—young Yossel went shopping as he usually
did. His new haircut made him stand out, and he could
hear everybody whispering behind his back, but he wasn't
ashamed. He quietly went about his chores: as oldest son it
was his duty to buy everything for Shabbes. I was visiting
Mirele and saw him hauling sacks and baskets into the house
filled with sugar, flour, raisins, oil, potatoes, and whatever
else the family of eleven needed for the holiday meal. Mirele
and I helped her mother put it all away and roll out the
dough for the cake. Yossel's mother had told him to buy
some things at Potok's little store to give that family a little
help, since the Potoks were so poor, they couldn't get any
credit from Dattelstrauch the wholesaler. For that reason
Yossel had to pay for his order two days in advance, on
Tuesday, so the Potoks could reserve what they needed
from Dattelstrauch on time. Then, on Thursday evening,

after Rivka Sheina came home from the shop, she stayed up past midnight baking and roasting the heavy tins filled with cake, fish, and meat for the Sabbath. But she didn't make the cholent until Friday morning. That's when she filled her large enameled pot with potatoes, meat, fat, barley, and beans—just the thing to make sure the whole family had enough for Saturday dinner.

"A good cholent has to bake for a whole day over a low fire. But of course Yossel's mother couldn't keep her oven burning straight through from Friday to Saturday, and neither could anyone else. For that reason everyone took their cholent pots to the baker's on Friday afternoon, so that by evening the oven there was packed with red, white, green, and yellow pots of different sizes, some round and broad and oval, some short and steep and tall. The richer families had thick cast-iron pots and often brought two, which the wiry short apprentice with a lazy left eye would shove in the middle of the oven—that was the best spot for baking. Then he'd set the thin pots of the poor people along the sides, where the cholent was in danger of burning. If that happened, the poor people were left with nothing, no matter how careful they'd been slicing the raw potatoes and glazing them with just the right amount of fat, then stacking them inside the pot and placing the meat with such artistry that it seemed the whole dish consisted of nothing but tasty, juicy bits of beef.

"There were also men so poor, all they could do was stand on the street and peer inside, hoping against hope for a small miracle that would enable them to send their

oldest child to the baker's next week, with a pot filled to
the brim.

"Yossel was ashamed of his family's cholent pot. The
inside was full of meat all right, but on the outside it looked
pitiful. Once upon a time it must have been a rich, even
brown, but now it was chipped and rusted and streaked
with black. The lid that fit it was missing and had been
replaced with another that always clattered loudly on the
stove. Yossel was so embarrassed, he packed the pot in old
newspapers before taking it to the baker's. During winter,
when the sun set early, he had to deliver the cholent by
three in the afternoon since the holiday began at sundown.
He also took a small pot of coffee for his father to drink the
next morning: on Saturday, before prayers, the devout Jews
drank their coffee at the baker's because they weren't
allowed to use their ovens at home on the Sabbath. So who
stoked the oven on Saturday mornings in the Hassidic bakery? After all, that was work, and work profaned the Sabbath. So who was it? The baker was devout, and of course
his apprentice Jonas was pious as well. But he was the one
they saddled with the dirty business, so he had to commit
a blasphemy every Saturday. After everyone, including the
baker, had left for the synagogue, Jonas would sit next to
the oven, dreaming of the bakery he might own someday,
with an apprentice like himself, who would also be annoyed
at having to work Saturdays. If he got bored he'd take a
few pots out of the oven—just for his own pleasure, as
though he were checking to make sure they were the right
temperature. He would pull out a pretty enameled pot and

lift the lid, and while his lazy eye could only discern the general outline, his healthy eye carefully inspected what kind of meat the rich Wassersteins would be eating that day and whether it was a good piece of beef, more tender than last Saturday, when it was still a little too tough even after the cholent had baked all day. He checked to see if the Goldsteins filled their pot like the Będziners or the way they did back in Vilna, where they had come from. And if the morning prayers went on a little long, and Jonas saw that the streets were still empty because all the passersby were in the synagogue, and if his dreams were slow in coming on that particular day, then he sometimes took the pots out of the oven and mixed up their contents, giving the lean pots a bit of meat from the fat ones, and the fat pots a few of the poor people's beans—a little compensation for this difficult, unfair life. But that hardly ever happened, because after all, where else could a poor apprentice who specialized in cholent and coffee expect to earn his keep other than in a little bakery tucked away in the heart of a Hassidic neighborhood?"

"LATER ON, IN the ghetto, handsome Adam was assigned to the same work detail as the cholent baker with the bad eyesight, and they worked shoulder to shoulder, hauling stones. With his usual ease Adam quickly picked up from Jonas the Yiddish that had once been so frowned upon in our school. One day the SS *Scharführer* called Adam out of the column and said, 'All right, you Jewish know-it-all, answer in German and not in your Jew-talk: what do you think now, which one of us is going to win the war, me or you?' Adam replied: 'Herr Scharführer, if you're planning to shoot me, then please do it right away. Because if I really say what I think, you'll shoot me, and if I say what you want to hear, you'll also shoot me.'

"The next day Adam was given a better assignment. But the cholent baker stayed in the same detail and because he had no one to speak on his behalf, he was selected for the first transport to Auschwitz. When they parted, Jonas told Adam he wasn't going to fight for his life: after all, even if he managed to survive, who would he bake cholent and make coffee for?"

"WHAT'S WRONG WITH you," Mrs. Kugelman asks, annoyed. "You're white as a ghost."

I'm overcome with anxiety. So many dead people.

Keep repeating it until you believe it, I tell myself. And that's exactly what I do: The streets of Będzin are mine, the people of Będzin are mine . . . And my father knew them all. And Gonna is my father. And sitting here in my room is Mrs. Kugelman, the one person left who knew him in his youth. I have to find out more.

"Mrs. Kugelman, you were right. Gonna, your class-mate, is my father!"

"So you say now, but what makes you so sure?"

"I just know it."

"When I said that two days ago, you wouldn't hear of it. And now you've decided to adopt him. As if it's up to you to choose your parents."

"Gonna is my father!"

"How can you be so shameless?" Mrs. Kugelman is getting angrier and angrier. "Who knows if the fish service is really yours in the first place? You'd never even heard of anyone named Bluma, and now you claim she was your grandmother. How dare you!"

"Bluma belongs to me."

"What do you mean 'belongs to you'! Is she your grandmother or not?"

"Yes," I shout, "she is!"

"You didn't even know her name."

"Father never told me. He never mentioned his mother."

Mrs. Kugelman is embarrassed and is silent for several minutes. Then she says, pensively: "So, you claim you're Gonna's daughter, or rather you want to be. Maybe you really are. Come here, let me take a look at you," she says, with a hint of kindness. Then she shakes her head in disbelief. "Who would have ever thought that someday I would meet Gonna's daughter," she mumbles quietly and looks me over a long time from head to toe.

"Do you see a resemblance?" I ask hopefully.

"I can't see any, but that doesn't mean anything. Think how many years it's been."

"I want to know everything about my father. Don't spare my feelings. Tell me everything. What he was like when he left Będzin? He was heartless and cold-blooded, wasn't he?" I pound her with questions.

I watch as her mouth twitches in pain.

"We're all tangled in guilt, not just your father. It sticks to our hands to this day. Even if we'd just been innocently stumbling along, today we're on trial all the time, sitting in the dock, face-to-face with ourselves, and not a day goes by when we don't think about it."

"Mrs. Kugelman, just tell me: could Father have sensed anything, back then in Będzin?"

"We knew the Germans treated their Jews badly, but no more than that. We lived very close to the border, and there were many people in Będzin who warned that war was coming soon. But no one suspected that the goal of this war would be our death."

She fixes her eyes on me, then turns away and goes on: "When Gonna left we went to the station and waved to him until his train rolled out of sight. We were filled with longing, and Kotek was in such despair about not going that he threw himself on the tracks and we had to drag him home.

"Kotek and I were the only ones from our class who'd actually seen firsthand what the Germans were doing to their Jews, although we had no idea that the same thing was in store for us. We saw it exactly one year before, in the middle of October, when Kotek's relatives arrived from Hannover."

17

‹o›

Venezuela slippers

"EARLIER THAT YEAR, KOTEK'S MOTHER HAD GIVEN HIM A
nice new pair of shoes—they looked like a real gentleman's, with a shiny toe-cap and fancy perforations. She
bought them a size too big, so they'd be a good fit by the
time the fall holidays came around. Kotek had great hopes
that his new shoes would make him look older, so he could
impress the proud Polish girl. But when I was over at his
house I noticed how his heels kept slipping out, so he took
a tape from his mother's sewing basket and asked me to
measure his feet, which were at least two centimeters too
short. I couldn't imagine he'd grow that much before the
fall, and told him to stuff some cotton gauze inside the toe,
but Kotek wouldn't do it. Instead he stole a bottle of castor
oil from his mother and rubbed it on his feet every day. Of
course the treatment didn't work—his feet didn't grow a
bit and, much to his dismay, he couldn't wear his new shoes
to the High Holidays. He was so upset he didn't want to

look at the new shoes, much less try putting them on. Then several weeks later he asked me to measure his feet again, and that happened to be same day his cousin Heinz arrived from Hannover.

"When Heinz stepped into Kotek's room, I was so horrified at his appearance that I dropped the measuring tape. He smelled awful, too. The buttons had been ripped off his shirt, he was sweaty and dirty, and his hair looked like it hadn't been combed in months. And his feet were so repulsive, I couldn't bear the sight of them. They seemed to be wrapped in grimy tattered rags—which he said had once been his slippers. He also had a curious way of placing his feet when he walked, as though he were trying to keep what was left of the slippers intact. Kotek had a very nice room, and Heinz clearly felt embarrassed when he stepped through the door.

"What could Kotek do? He was sad but he had to give up the shoes he'd never worn. And Heinz had no choice either—he had to accept the gift or else go barefoot. I could tell he was ashamed to the point of tears, which he kept wiping away when he thought no one was looking.

"The Kanners arrived in Będzin in October—I remember it was a bitterly cold day. Apart from Heinz there were his two sisters, Betti and Anni, his parents, Liane and Herbert, and his singing grandmother, Lena. They didn't have anything more than the clothes on their backs. Heinz was probably the only person on the train wearing slippers. Early that morning in Hannover, men in heavy boots had kicked down the door and screamed at his family that they had ten minutes to get dressed. In all the chaos it wasn't easy to find anything, and Heinz didn't have time to look for his leather shoes. His parents didn't realize he was still in his slippers when they were chased to the station.

"The slippers were a present from his mother's younger brother, Uncle Solly, who was, believe it or not, only three years older than Heinz. Solly had left for Venezuela a few months earlier and given Heinz his slippers since he wouldn't be needing them there. Venezuela was so warm and tropical, you could run around barefoot even in the morning. And if it did get cold, then a beautiful woman with fiery eyes would warm his feet—at least that's what Solly told Heinz. Moreover, in Venezuela you could sleep through the night without fear. And in the morning you could bite into a hefty slice of bread smeared so thick with good Venezuelan butter that your teeth would leave a mark. In Venezuela you could eat two or three butter sandwiches without worrying you were depriving other family members of the small portion that Jews were allotted.

"The slippers were comfortable and attractive. On the outside they were gray, inside they were lined with white fabric, and in front they had a nice furry cuff that curved off to the side and toward the front like a tiny coat collar. They kept Heinz's feet warm and cozy. Whenever he wore them, he felt he was with Uncle Solly in Venezuela.

"And so Heinz climbed onto the train wearing his Venezuela slippers, prodded by a rifle stock because the loading wasn't going fast enough. In all the hubbub he got separated from his family. But he knew they were somewhere in the rear of the car because he could hear his father, Herbert Kanner, calling out his name as the train started moving.

"Heinz had never been on a train like this one—there were no seats of any kind. So many people had been shoved inside that everyone had to stand jammed together except for some old and sick people and a few children— fortunately there weren't too many of those—who sat or lay on the cold floor, one on top of the other, hardly moving. Heinz was crammed up toward the front, right next to a tiny window.

"The whole car smelled of livestock, and Heinz's eyes stung and his nose ran just like it did on the meadow during summer. And because his slippers were so thin, Heinz could feel the straw on the floor and everything other people's feet were doing. To his right a man used his legs to help steady a small woman who cried out in fear when the train passed over some switches. Heinz could tell that they didn't know each other, because the man stepped back right away, so as not to touch her. When we reached a road crossing he did the same thing. This went on for a long time, until finally, after several bumpy stretches the man and the woman let their feet rub against each other just for a little human comfort.

"To Heinz's left a frail man was prepared to kick anyone who came too near. When people realized he was holding a small child, they gave him a little space so that he and the child wouldn't get jostled every time the train rounded a bend.

"But then all of a sudden two tall men pushed right up to Heinz and stomped on his slippers with all their weight. He cried out in pain and they stomped on him again. The rivets from the fur collar dug into his flesh, and his right foot began to swell. Heinz had no idea what the men were after. Then they packed him by the arm and shoved him backward, causing several people to fall. Only after he got back on his feet did Heinz realize that the two men wanted his place by the window.

"The tiny opening let in a little fresh air, and that was very welcome since the stench in the car was getting worse and worse. But the best thing about the window was that you could see the world outside and tell by the station signs where the train was headed. And that was east, toward Poland.

"You see, all the people in the car were Jews with Polish passports who had been living in Germany—although it took a while before they figured out what they had in common. Some of them, like Heinz, had never even been to Poland. He was born in Germany and didn't speak a word of Polish, but he was registered under his father's Polish passport. His family had planned to get out of Germany and join Uncle Solly in Caracas, and they were waiting for their Venezuelan visas when they were rousted out of bed and loaded onto the train.

"Herbert Kanner saw the commotion and shouted for Heinz to move to the back of the car. But Heinz didn't answer because he was afraid of getting trampled again, so his father pushed his way forward and finally made it through. When he saw the slippers and the blood on Heinz's right foot, without saying a word he lifted his son off his slippered feet and onto his own.

"The trains traveled right up to the Polish border but didn't cross into Zbąszyń, the first town in Poland. Instead they simply dumped their cargo just short of the border, like a sack of rotten potatoes nobody in Germany wanted anymore—and the Poles didn't want either. The empty cars returned to Germany for the next transport, and the people who'd been thrown out were driven with rifle shots into Poland on foot. Heinz's grandfather was hit and killed during the process. The family couldn't even tend to his body because the Germans kept firing and shouting: Keep moving, keep moving, you Jewish swine! When Heinz's grandmother Lena refused to go on, his father lifted her up and tossed her over his shoulder. She screamed that she couldn't leave her husband lying there, and tried to break away, but Herbert Kanner held her tight and wouldn't let her down.

"From then on Grandmother Lena couldn't go anywhere unless she was carried. As soon as her feet touched the earth she would start to rave; she couldn't get the image out of her mind of her husband's body, just lying there on the ground. When she was carried, though, she calmed down, and she could even be quite clearheaded. Of course Heinz's father couldn't carry her all the time, and Heinz himself could barely walk, so his two younger sisters, Betti and Anni, formed a sling and took their grandmother in the middle. Lena wrapped her arms around the girls and used them for support. The swaying gait did her good, and she even began to sing. She had a beautiful high voice and sang old songs, both sad and happy, all in the same pitch, as though she were once again a young girl, facing her life that lay ahead, full of hope.

"So the family trudged several kilometers to Zbąszyń, carrying their singing grandmother. The farmers along the way gave them bread and milk, but Lena wouldn't eat so much as a crumb, she just kept on singing, even after they finally got on board the regular train that took them to Będzin.

"As soon as they arrived they brought Lena upstairs to see Dr. Goldstaub, who gave her a thorough examination. After he put down his stethoscope, he turned to the family and told them the sad news that Lena didn't have long to live. Her pulse was critically slow, and her ability to supply blood severely compromised. The Kanners had their doubts about the diagnosis, but as usual, Dr. Goldstaub was right, and Lena passed away just a few days later."

18

━◆━

Eleven months

"By the time the Kanners arrived in Będzin, the town had exactly eleven months left. The evil out of Germany was coming closer and closer, and the trains from Zbąszyń brought more and more deportees. The rabbi of Czeladź—that was a small town about four kilometers outside of Będzin—called on his congregation to help the refugees in their great need. But the people there were so poor they had nothing to give, so the rabbi told his followers to break the commandment and work on the Sabbath instead of resting. Whatever they earned could help save the refugees. At the time nobody realized how soon they'd be facing similar circumstances and that in less than a year Hitler would ruin their lives as well.

"Those eleven months flew by at an incredible speed—faster than any other time I can remember. And all the while, life in Będzin went on more or less as usual.

"Seven and a half months before the Germans invaded,

at two thirty in the afternoon, after three failed attempts, Rivka Sheina finally managed to solve the riddle of the ingredients for the Thursday cheesecake. Six and a half months before the invasion, Dattelstrauch the wholesaler collapsed with an ulcer a few days after his young wife left him. Rumor had it that she'd been spotted at the Łódź train station, arm in arm with Professor Rado. Five months before the invasion, Teitelbaum stopped traveling to Katowice because he couldn't sell his coats: from one day to the next the farmers started avoiding his store. Two weeks later Rabinowicz raised the fee for the last book from Warsaw. In protest, some of the students stopped going to his store and began using the school library, much to the joy of our principal.

"In June, three months before the invasion, Kotek, Mietek, Gonna, the Polish girl, and I were busy preparing for our state exams and had no time for anything else. The students in the grades just below us continued to sneak out of class as usual. And if life had gone on the way it always had, come September even our youngest schoolmates would have learned how to play hooky by the river. But they never had a chance because when the Germans took over, one of the first things they did was shut down the schools.

"Just before that happened, though, the town was buzzing with a scandal involving a good friend of Kotek's named Meyer, who had finished school with the rest of us—although just barely. He was a tall, handsome boy who spent more time playing cards than doing homework.

Most of his grades were pretty bad, but he did very well in Latin because he wanted to make an impression on the teacher Fanny Sternenlicht—and he clearly managed to do that. Thanks to his high score in Latin he passed his state exam, and, as far as Fanny Sternenlicht was concerned, that also qualified him to be her husband. Meyer didn't want to put things off, and the two got married, much to the disgrace of his parents. Three days later the Germans were in Będzin, and the new regulations posted on every building made it a crime for us to go to school, and anyone who disobeyed could face the death penalty.

"And so the Fürstenberg Gymnasium became a collection point for confiscated goods. That's what they called the things they stole from us: fur coats, clothing, radios, bicycles, and hats. The items were sorted in our classrooms, and anything of any value was sent to Germany. Adam made fun of the Germans for wearing the same clothes he had worn next to his skin—after all, according to the new laws coming out of Berlin, people could be sent to prison for race defilement if they touched certain parts of a naked Jewish body—even just one single time."

I WAKE UP early the next morning and open the window to my room. For the very first time I feel the khamsin, the wind that sometimes blows in from the desert, plunging the city into an oppressive yellow-gray cloud. I taste the sand on my tongue. The whole city wheezes and groans in the humid heat. Everyone is on edge.

I'm worked up as well.

Mrs. Kugelman steps into my room and loosens the headscarf she's wrapped around her mouth. She coughs and says something about the dust storm as she takes her seat.

"I'm not interested in the dust storm. I want to know what we're doing in the middle of the war—I thought we'd agreed you were just going to talk about the good times, when everything was peaceful!"

"Peaceful times give way to war," she answers curtly. She sits up straight in her chair. "I can't spare you."

"Have you ever spared anybody?" I say, feeling anger welling inside me.

"My children."

"You have children?"

"Two boys. They long since have families of their own."

"You didn't tell them anything?"

"No!"

A woman who can't stop telling stories about her town, and she didn't tell her own children a thing?

"Not even something completely harmless, for instance about Malka Feiga the schnorrer or Lachman the barber?" I ask suspiciously.

"No. I never once mentioned the word Będzin."

"Do your children even know where you were born?"

"They never asked."

"Even when they were little? They never said, 'Mama show me the house where you grew up'?"

"No."

Maybe your sons didn't ask any questions because they

knew they wouldn't get any answers, I thought. I didn't ask
my parents either: I didn't even know I could have.

"And later on, once they were grown up, they didn't
ask any questions then either?"

"My sons didn't ask, and I didn't tell. I didn't want them
to grow up with all that death and despair."

"But at some point they must have been old enough to
take the truth! You ought to have told them."

"We spared one another." She wipes away a tear, speaking so quietly that I have to lean in to hear her. "They
didn't want to make me cry. They knew I would have broken into pieces at my own words. My children realized
that without my ever having said anything about it."

Mrs. Kugelman's children somehow understood what
their mother needed. They didn't ask questions but they
still managed to show their affection. And what about me?
I think about how I treated my parents. When they were
silent I kept my distance. And yet I was their child; I came
from their blood and skin and bones. It wasn't just their
silence that kept us apart: I'm the one who locked myself in
my frozen world.

"Do your children know what's going on here in my
room?" I ask kindly, taking her hand. I want her to let me
put my arms around her and hug her the way I'd never
hugged my own parents.

"No, they don't know anything."

"You have given me so much, more than you've given
your own children. Doesn't that bother you?"

"It does," she says sadly, and looks off into the distance.

"Perhaps all survivors should tell their stories to someone else's children, because it's so hard to speak to your own."

We pass a moment in silence.

"Then thousands would travel to Israel from all over the world, all the children who want to know everything their parents couldn't bear to tell them," I say hoarsely. "They'll gather in little clusters around park benches or in cafés or on the beach—wherever the storytellers tell their tales. All other divisions will vanish. There will no longer be rich and poor, young and old, man and woman—only those who listen and those who tell."

She nods, smiles gently, and gives me a friendly look. "Just like the two of us in this hotel room."

Then she again turns away, leans heavily back into her chair, and picks up where she left off the day before.

19

Boycott Silesians

"NOW EVEN AFTER THE KANNERS SHOWED UP IN BĘDZIN looking the way they did, if someone had told us that within a few months the Germans would kick us out of our own school we would have roared with laughter. But in hindsight, there'd been warning signs for years. I remember one day in sixth grade when Moniek showed up with some paper forms he'd smuggled out of his house. They were ballots that his father, Romek Ziegler, had printed up for a large meeting he was calling in their apartment. My father made special plans to attend, and took the train in from Zawiercie. I met him at the station and told him what we'd heard from Moniek. It was a big secret, but Father laughed out loud when I mentioned that Romek Ziegler was planning to add some drama by taking his best jacket, which had been custom tailored in Berlin at the famous Dilling atelier, and burning it in the kitchen stove, just to put the guests in the right mood. Moniek had also told us that his father often opened the meetings with some kind of theatrical gesture, after which everybody would start talking at once, very loudly. Then all of a sudden the men would quiet down to take a vote. His father would count hands and, depending on the outcome, some of the participants would stand up and applaud while others walked out grumbling."

"ROMEK ZIEGLER WAS very experienced when it came to secret meetings. This time he had invited his fellow industrialists—mostly steel manufacturers and iron merchants—to discuss what to do about the horrible anti-Semite from Austria who'd recently taken over all of Germany. A number of them came, too, but not as many as he'd hoped, and he was so mad at the ones who didn't come that he decided to cut them out of any future business dealings, and he had dealings in just about everything. But before he presented any proposals he wanted to make clear to his colleagues the dangers lurking next door in Germany, and this wasn't easy, since all the manufacturers had so many business ties there. For a while they sat and chatted over vodka, but at one point Romek Ziegler stood up and turned on the radio, which was tuned to a nearby German station. The men listened to the hoarse rise and fall of the ranting, and when they heard the thunderous applause that followed each of the Austrian's declarations, the living room went quiet—far too quiet as far as Moniek was concerned. He was afraid, scared of what the voice in the radio had to say.

"Romek Ziegler urged his guests to action. After all, they lived in Będzin, right next to the border, they couldn't shut their eyes, they had to do something for their brothers in Germany, and also for the Jews of Poland. They couldn't simply look the other way while the government of such an important country drove Jewish professionals out of every single line of work and publically portrayed all Jews as parasites sucking the blood of Germans.

"What was particularly frightening was how much support Hitler had won just across the border, among the same German Silesians the Będziners did so much business with. But enough was enough, and now was the time and here was the place, according to Romek Ziegler. The Będziners couldn't act as if nothing had happened, he declared. They should take a stand, set an example, and organize a boycott of Silesian goods.

"'Let them sit on their inventory!' he shouted. 'Let them sit on their tin, their lead, their zinc, their steel!'

"Lowering his voice, he went on: 'Believe me, gentlemen, if we, the Jewish steel merchants of Będzin, boycott their wares, word will soon reach Herr Hitler in Berlin, and this, my friends, will hit him hard!'

"Here he took a little pause for dramatic effect.

"'Our next step will be to take the boycott to other cities, first to Łódź, where all Jewish textile manufacturers need to stop ordering their machines from Chemnitz and Gleiwitz. One by one, the German cities will grind to a halt. And soon'—here his voice rose again—'the boycott will spread all across Poland and strike Hitler to the marrow!'

"It took more than one meeting for Romek Ziegler to get the support he wanted, but he refused to give up, and eventually he won over enough of the manufacturers and town dignitaries to put the boycott into practice.

"Replacing the German wares was not an easy task, and the manufacturers had to make sure they had enough pipes and iron wheels and copper and tin on hand to keep their factories running. New business partners had to be found who were as punctual and careful with their deliveries as the Silesians. Romek Ziegler, who had studied engineering in Lille, determined that Czechoslovakian products were the next best thing and drove to Prague to order the raw materials. His plan was to set up a local factory that would produce the machines and tools previously purchased in Silesia—as well as the replacement parts, in case some little cog went missing. He also consulted with several chemists, including my father in Zawiercie.

"Soon Frenkel and Süssmann and the other manufacturers began ordering from Czechoslovakia and even from Vienna, although that had once been the home of the fanatical Nazi chancellor. Fürstenberg also stopped buying from the Germans, but he chose not to put up any money for Romek Ziegler's new factory because his eyes didn't stop tearing up when he visited the site.

"As the months went on, Moniek lost all interest in the boycott, worried as he was about his friendship with Max and Erna Matussek, who lived right over border. Moniek had been looking forward to going on summer vacation with them to the Giant Mountains, which he very much wanted to see on account of Rübezahl and his seven-league boots. He asked his father if they could still be friends, but all Romek Ziegler said was that he was sorry: Matussek was his friend, too, but the trade stoppage meant that the business relationship was over, and no one could say whether the friendship would last.

"It wasn't long, though, before the boycott ran into trouble. For one thing, the long transport meant heavy shipping costs, which in turn cut into each company's profits. The smaller merchants were especially hard hit and many of them had to close their business. In that way the boycott ruined several families overnight.

"There were also people who chose to undercut the boycott. And some of them made a lot of money. In particular I'm thinking of the Teitelbaum brothers Samek and Poldek, who were always on the lookout for jobs that might help them put food on the table. They'd listened to the same rants on the radio as everybody else, but they weren't so concerned about the applause that followed. When they got wind of the boycott of German goods they smelled a way to make some money, and when they learned that Mordechai's shoe factory had run out of a special type of nail, they crossed the border on foot, made their way to Beuthen, and returned with a sackful of nails. Another time they picked up some cheap remnants from a hat store that went out of business and started looking for a buyer. Everybody seemed to need something, and soon the brothers signed on a few Bachmans, who were clearly suffering because of the boycott, as well as a few coachmen who were loitering around the train station with no employment. These men would wait until it was pitch-dark and then they'd drive their carts across the border. And after midnight, when the whole town was asleep, they'd bring the Silesian goods back to Będzin. The brothers made it very easy for their clients by delivering zinc and steel, brass and silver, pots and pans, shovels and shears cheaply and comfortably right to the door.

"And so, all of a sudden, the Teitelbaum brothers were rich, and their women summoned Rivka Sheina, Mirele's mother, to the third rear courtyard, much to the envy of their neighbors, and had her make up some fine clothes for their children. They also had the cobbler make each child a brand-new pair of soft leather shoes. Leah Dresel's even had a little heel, since she was the oldest. Day and night the one table they possessed was piled high with good food, and they distributed the leftovers to their neighbors who were just as poor as they had been.

"There was yet another reason why the boycott lost steam and ultimately faded away, and that had to do with all the close personal ties. Even Romek Ziegler was not unaffected, although he held out the longest. No one wanted to admit it, but the truth was that each of the Będzin industrialists had his own Silesian, so to speak—people they'd been dealing with for years, business partners they trusted, whose word was a valid contract, whose goods were top quality, and who in the rare case of complaint would take back the items sold with no grumbling and promptly replace the defective item with a good one. Over time these partnerships became more personal, and the Silesian children played with the children in Będzin.

"Everyone had his Silesian, and everyone was willing to swear that his Silesian wasn't a Nazi and would never become a Nazi in a hundred years. Romek Ziegler's Silesian was the same Matussek whose children were such good friends of Moniek. Matussek was a man of his word, punctual, exact, and reliable, and Romek was certain that he considered the Nazis a band of primitive thugs. What was perhaps even more amazing was that each of the Silesians had his Jew, with whom he continued to do business. And Matussek could vouch to his German colleagues that Romek Ziegler was very different than the Jews Hitler talked about. He was reliable, punctual, and exact, in short, a man of his word by German standards—except Matussek didn't say that out loud because you never knew what the times would bring.

"So, long after the Teitelbaums had undercut the boycott, and long after the other merchants had resumed buying from their Silesians, Romek Ziegler finally placed first one new order with Matussek and then another and then a whole series of orders.

"Once the merchants went back to ordering from their Silesians, it wasn't long before the Teitelbaum brothers grew poor again. They ran through their newfound wealth so fast, their women never had time to have Rivka Sheina stitch up clothes for themselves, since they'd ordered clothes for the children first. Once again they had to buy things on credit from Potok the grocer, and each month they had to ask if they could defer payment. The two brothers were back on the street, alert for any job, and everything went on just as it had before.

"At least that's how it seemed. The truth is that even though the boycott ran its course, and the Będziners resumed doing business with the Silesians, few of the old friendships survived the years that followed.

"It happened very slowly. First some official Reich decree was enacted against a Jewish conspiracy or some other idiocy—it was amazing what even educated, grown-up people were willing to believe—with the result that the Silesians no longer wanted to do business with the Będzin merchants. Letters passed back and forth, but goods weren't delivered on time, and orders were no longer accepted. The Fürstenbergs, Frenkels, and Süssmanns noticed the changes and withdrew their business and then, from one day to the next, the friendships were over.

"Only Matussek acted differently. He was honest with Moniek's father and told him straight out he could no longer deliver orders as punctually as before because the raw material was urgently needed in the Reich. He also mentioned that two very properly attired gentlemen had been inquiring for some time whether the Jew Romek Ziegler was supplying weapons factories in Chorzów with German steel, and because of their questions Matussek thought it best not to sell Romek any more steel.

"Finally, in early June 1939, Matussek traveled to Będzin for a serious conversation with Romek. He started off by telling his friend that he'd recently joined the Nazi Party.

His brother-in-law Fritz had joined long ago and was now a high-ranking member. Fritz owned a small textile mill in Lauban that produced cloth for handkerchiefs, but recently he'd switched over to manufacturing cloth for uniforms. Fritz told Matussek it would be advantageous if the whole family were members and urged his father-in-law to join. Matussek did as he was asked, and as soon as he did, Fritz received a huge order for cloth production, as well as a number of commissions for tailoring uniforms to be worn by leading party members. For that reason Matussek had decided to shift his business, because a big war was coming and there was a lot of money to be made off uniforms.

"But that wasn't the only thing, Matussek said. He and his son-in-law had gone to Berlin to discuss materials and cuts for different uniforms, and there they met several high-ranking military officers who spoke openly about plans to attack Poland and were certain that German tanks and airplanes would guarantee a quick victory. And because the Jews in the east were even more a thorn in the side than they were in the Reich, they would have to be cleared away. Matussek had learned from Fritz that Moniek's father was at the top of a blacklist prepared by ethnic Germans living in Poland because of the steel he was delivering to Chorzów. So now Matussek was begging his friend to flee or else they'd never see each other again, at least not in this life.

"Moniek's father decided to leave as soon as possible. But this time he didn't call a meeting—there wasn't any point: after all, you can't vote on whether a whole town should flee in case of invasion. He told the town leaders about his plans, and everything went very quickly. The family didn't take anything that wasn't absolutely necessary—mostly clothing for the coming winter. In case the Germans did conquer Poland—which no one was ready to believe—the family would flee farther east, into Russia.

"Moniek was delighted that they chose to leave when they did because Fanny Sternenlicht had announced a Latin test for the following morning. He would have been upset if a move like that had interrupted his summer vacation, but as it was he was more than happy to help his parents, and he loaded the horse cart with cool drinks for that hot June day. He was convinced his family would return to Będzin after everything had calmed down and that he'd be sharing a desk with his friend Mietek by the beginning of the school year. But in all the commotion of leaving, he forgot about his important job as treasurer of the Rapid Sport Club and failed to name a successor in his absence, someone who could reliably manage the money—Gonna, for instance, or Marysia Teitelbaum, if need be, since the girl was neat and good at arithmetic. And so all the money from the membership dues stayed sealed in an airtight iron cash box inside Moniek's carved wooden drawer and wasn't multiplying the way good capital should. The keys to the drawer and the box were bunched together in Moniek's pants pocket, but he didn't realize it until they were halfway to the Ukraine. Then he felt horrible. How could the club function? How could they pay for new membership cards and trophies? And worst of all, everyone except his best friend, Mietek, would say that he had taken the box for himself, that he stole all the money. The keys jingled and jangled inside his pocket at every bump in the road, as if they were deliberately trying to remind him of his mistake.

"Their first stop was Tarnów, where they were put up in a nice hotel by the company Heinzel and Son, who still owed Romek Ziegler money for a shipment. The family felt safe in Tarnów and decided to stay there as long as they needed. But after the Germans invaded Będzin, they had to climb back on their horse cart and hurry farther east—all because of the Germans' list.

"A few days after leaving Tarnów, Moniek made a discovery so gruesome he forgot all about the cash box. The family had stopped to catch their breath in a small village outside Lwów, and someone told them about another refugee from Będzin—a teacher who'd come back to her home and was living with her parents. Of course there were many schools in Będzin, but Moniek hoped it would be a teacher from Fürstenberg. He missed his school so much, he would have been happy to see anyone, including Kowalski the custodian or even Fanny Sternenlicht—in fact, he would have loved to make up his Latin test right then and there on the meadow. He found out where the refugee was living, and as he approached the house he saw a woman sitting on the grass, completely motionless, as if she were dead. When he went a little closer she turned her head and stuck her tongue out at him. It was Pani Kleinowa. Moniek had never seen her tongue before: it was narrow in front and broad in the middle, rosy on the sides, and a normal white coating in the back—even Dr. Goldstaub would have said it looked healthy. But for Moniek it was such a shock to see his Polish teacher sticking her tongue out that he started to cry. 'Pani Kleinowa,' he asked gently, 'is there something I can do for you?' She didn't answer him but went on sticking out her tongue, as if there were nothing to say, and then her old father came and led her inside, without asking Moniek who he was or if he knew his daughter from when she was a teacher."

"Did she ever recover?"

"That was the last I heard of her. We all know she was a nervous type—she used to drive us crazy. She'd tell us to look into her eyes and say that if they were blue, then she wouldn't give us a lot of homework. But her eyes were always blue, and still she assigned a lot of homework and she was very strict about it, too. She was full of little quirks like that. But what Moniek saw was different. Her nerves had been completely shattered by what she had witnessed in Będzin."

20

◄o►

When they came

"EVEN IN THESE WORST OF TIMES, OUR HASSIDIM STILL believed in miracles. The day before the German soldiers crossed the border, Mendel and his family left Będzin: in moments like that everyone's first priority was to get their families to safety. They closed down their store, and in their apartment they covered the armchairs with white sheets, drew the shutters, and bolted the front door. Mendel grabbed one blanket for each member of his family, and Rivka Sheina packed a basket with chicken fat and bread. They slipped out through the back door and headed into the forest. On their way they met Gabłoński the pharmacist, who lent them his horse cart. They could have chosen any number of small towns, since they had relatives throughout the area, but Mendel wanted to be close to his rebbe, who had fled east, to Olkusz. There they spent the night in a tiny room crowded with other families fleeing the Germans, and they all talked about what to do next.

Everybody agreed that only the men were in danger and that the women and children would be safe from any harm. The men decided to make their way to Russia—the only question was whether they should take their families or not: after all, it was a long, hard journey. Mendel weighed the options but couldn't make up his mind, so he decided to consult with his rebbe. The old man thought for a moment and then told Mendel that he should leave Olkusz without delay and take his family back west to Dąbrowa. They should travel as quickly as possible and not stop even for a minute. So they reloaded their bags onto the cart and set off together with some other refugee families from Będzin. When they reached Sławków they ran into Gutka Fürstenberg with her Christian husband and Shlomo Fürstenberg with his wife, Mania, and their three small children, as well as the Teitelbaum brothers and their four sons, all of whom were desperately searching for Poldek's daughter Leah Dresel, who'd somehow managed to get separated from her family. They also saw Mietek—his entire family was on the move and had stopped in Sławków to buy provisions and rest a little from their journey. Mirele wanted to do the same, but her father wouldn't hear of it. Holding her arm so hard it hurt, he led his family across what was left of the bridge that had been demolished by the retreating Polish troops and didn't let go until they were safely on the other side. Just before they arrived in Strzemieszyce they heard the sound of motors and guns but, mindful of the rebbe's warning, they kept going as fast as they could, without stopping for even a second to catch their breath.

"The next morning Mendel learned that when the invaders reached Sławków they rounded up Jewish men and cut their beards off just for amusement. Afterward the Germans fired at the Jews struggling to cross the ruined bridge—just like they were targets at a shooting range—killing them with a single shot in the back. The dead bodies were tossed into the little river, which was no larger than our own, and soon the shallow, brownish water ran red with blood. Rado was among them, floating downstream, his ugly face hidden from view. Before the Germans shot him he had sung louder than he'd ever sung before—an eerie melody that pierced through all the rumbling of trucks and gunfire. And in that way he managed to distract the attention of the soldiers just long enough for the four red-haired Teitelbaum sons to escape to the forest."

"WHEN THEY REACHED Dąbrowa, Mendel and his family spent the night in a large apartment belonging to an old aunt whose children had long since moved to Palestine. Mirele, Yossel, and the other plump siblings had never had so much space.

"Despite everything they'd seen and heard, Mendel still hadn't lost his faith in the Germans. He remembered how during the First World War German soldiers had rescued women and children from burning buildings. He refused to believe that this war could possibly be that different. How could such a cultivated nation change overnight?

"But the Germans had no intention of making a detour

just for Mendel's sake, and so their army marched on into Dąbrowa. Shortly before dusk, when the men were about to go to prayers, there was a deafening noise, and the family turned out all the lights and took shelter in the cellar. Only Mirele stayed upstairs, much to her parents' horror, wrapping herself in a curtain, her eyes peering out of the flowery fabric like two little brown buttons. No soldier looking up from the street would have suspected that a curious young girl was hiding by the window.

"Afterward, when she was pressed for details, Mirele reported that the German army hadn't looked very different from the Polish army, except the trucks and guns seemed a little newer and everything was painted bluish green. There weren't any horses or cavalry, either. But the two motorcyclists riding in advance of the column were the most terrifying thing she'd ever witnessed. She'd never seen men so big—they must have been specially selected to scare the poor Jews. They'd raced through the streets wearing uniforms black as ravens, with huge helmets and black-rimmed goggles, rolling over everything that stood in their way.

"Her family kept asking her to repeat what she'd seen, and with every retelling the men on the motorcycles grew a little bigger, until they finally turned into giants with tall black boots who roared by on their huge machines, randomly darting this way and that to shoot a few pedestrians from the curb before returning to the head of the marching column. They seemed not humans but hounds of hell come to enslave and kill the Jews, just like in the time of Moses. Mirele closed her eyes and she knew for certain that this time there would be no God to part the Red Sea and lead his people to safety, and that all her nearest and dearest would sink along with her in a great sea of burning fire.

"And when she opened her eyes once more, she was no longer a child. She was exactly as tall as she'd been the moment before, with the same eyes, the same hair, the same voice, but she felt so terribly old, as if she were the oldest person in the world, a thousand years older than Methuselah."

EVERYTHING HAS GOTTEN very quiet, as if the room and whole hotel and the entire city were listening to Mrs. Kugelman.

"They came early on the morning of September fourth, when the air was still cool and fresh. I don't think they realized they were marching into a ghost town. All doors were locked, all gates were latched, and all the people who made their living on the street—the shills and schnorrers, the Bachmans and coachmen, the peddlers and vendors— were hiding inside, watching and waiting.

"Marysia Teitelbaum's parents had forbidden her to walk Kajtuś that day, but against their wishes she'd opened the front door just a crack to let the poodle out. The dog ran through the empty streets, returning home long before the soldiers arrived. So by the time the German soldiers came marching down Małachowski Street there was nothing but dead silence—and a dotty old woman standing next to an excited blond girl with long, thick braids.

"The dotty old woman was Mrs. Żmigród and the excited blond girl was me. We were standing on the street, welcoming the soldiers to Będzin.

"I had actually planned to go back to Zawiercie that morning. The trains were still running, and I wanted to get there as early as possible, since my parents were so worried. But just before dawn we heard a great rattling and rumbling from the motorcycles and trucks and heavy caterpillar tractors hauling artillery. I looked out the window and saw more soldiers than I'd ever seen on Małachowski Street.

"Mrs. Żmigród accompanied me outside and helped me with my suitcase. We waited for a gap between the columns of infantry so I could cross the street and get to the station. But the men kept marching, one after the other, and we stood there for an hour without moving. And then Mrs. Żmigród began waving at the soldiers. All of a sudden they were no longer an invading army but romantic heroes, just like the ones pictured in my German schoolbooks that Mrs. Żmigród read when I was out—handsome men in dashing uniforms, marching in perfect step. She would have liked best to have given them a piece of the cheesecake she'd baked especially as a treat for my family.

"'Welcome, *meine Herren*, to Będzin,' she said to the soldiers, and since no one answered, she called out louder and louder until the neighbors heard her from behind their closed windows and shouted for us to run upstairs as fast as we could before the men started firing.

"But they didn't fire at all: in fact I didn't hear a single shot in Będzin. For four whole days everything was peaceful— the only difference was that the Polish garrison had disappeared, no one knew where to. I asked a neighbor who had a store in Zawiercie to let my parents know that the war wasn't so bad and that I'd go on staying with Mrs. Żmigród.

"That first day some of the soldiers even exchanged a few words with us at the rynek. Then, on the evening of the second day, they knocked on Lachman's barbershop with the butts of their rifles. Lachman quickly covered his two oldest daughters with sheets and hid them under the bed. But the soldiers were only after money and clothing, and left once they got what they wanted.

"On the third day, the people who had fled began coming back, including Mendel and his family. They reported that the whole region had been occupied and that several people had been killed.

"The fourth day started off peacefully, but on that evening—it was Friday, September eighth—the war against us broke out in full force. In the dark we could see smoke coming out of the synagogue. We climbed onto the roof and saw that the synagogue, the surrounding houses, and the entire neighborhood were burning.

"The Germans had surrounded the area and forced men, women, and children into the synagogue and then set it on fire. No wonder Pani Kleinowa had been driven mad at such a sight.

"That same night Mendel came to Mrs. Żmigród's. Tears were streaming down his face. His voice faltered as he told his sister-in-law about visiting his sick mother in Sosnowiec, where he saw the synagogue burn. He heard that the Germans were setting fire to all the synagogues in the region, and he hurried home because he was worried about his family who lived so close to the one in Będzin. Maybe the Germans have gone mad, he thought, maybe they're determined to see every synagogue burn no matter where. As he came closer, he saw that the Christians who lived in the neighborhood were making a point of crossing themselves so that the Germans would spare them. When he reached his street it was more horrible than he could put into words. His house had been set on fire, and his wife and eight children had tried to escape but had been driven back into the burning building. Yossel had jumped from the window and was shot in midair.

"Mendel told Mrs. Żmigród that he couldn't get their voices out of his mind. He said he kept hearing them calling out to him—his wife; Yossel, his oldest son; Mirele; each one of his eight children—begging him to save them from the flames, their voices slowly fading away, until all that was left were their tiny, desperate, suffocated cries. And then it would start all over again.

"The next day, as soon as it was light, I set out for Zawiercie on foot. The train was no longer running. It was a long way away, but I only stopped once or twice to catch my breath. I didn't tell Mrs. Żmigród good-bye—I was so mad at her for having welcomed the soldiers. And I was equally mad at myself for just standing there and not doing anything. I should have wished that Małachowski Street would split open and swallow the invading army and that every last man and every truck and gun and cannon would sink into the bowels of the earth and never again see the light of day. Perhaps, if I'd wished that strong enough, I could have saved us from our great misfortune."

I REFILL MRS. KUGELMAN'S glass and she drinks very slowly, carefully setting it on the table between swallows. She sips her water while I gulp down her words, which course through my veins and fill me with new energy, new purpose. But Mrs. Kugelman is visibly weakened, to the point of exhaustion. Earlier I had noticed she was using an umbrella as a walker. She seems too vain to carry a cane. I help her downstairs, force her to ride the elevator. Drained, she closes her eyes and grabs hold of me when the elevator jerks into motion. In the hotel lobby I ask her to sit on the sofa for a moment before going home and gently hold her arm.

"I want to help you," I tell her.

Mrs. Kugelman shakes off my hand. "I don't need you," she says.

"Let me work with you to save your town."

Her round body straightens up, and her eyes flash with anger, as if her old strength were coming back.

"Keep your fingers out of this," she says.

"With my help you can reach twice as many people."

"That's enough. Leave the telling to us."

"I can repeat what you've told me—your words, your sentences, your stories."

"Don't try to be me."

"Everything I say will be through your eyes. Trust me."

"Trust has nothing to do with it. It's a question of truth. And you can't tell the truth unless you were there. Unless you saw Będzin with your own eyes."

"But what happens when there's no one left from Będzin?"

"I don't know. Maybe everything will simply be forgotten."

"You can't say that. You have to believe in a future. Make me your apprentice so I can take over when the time comes. Teach me how to tell your stories!"

"I've already told you: keep your fingers out of this!"

Glaring at me, she stands up as if there's nothing more to say and, leaning on her umbrella, drags herself to the revolving door.

I STAND THERE, shunned, abandoned, ashamed. I need to get out of here. Upstairs in my room I pack my things as fast as I can and call Koby, sobbing. I ask him to reserve a room in a different hotel, he takes me there in his taxi, carries my suitcase, negotiates the price for me at the reception desk. The clerk smiles as he hands me the key. And I smile back. Tonight I will not think of Mrs. Kugelman.

When I step inside my new room, the first thing I see is the refrigerator. I wonder if I should remove the ice cube tray as a precaution, but when I open the door to the freezer the cold streaming out doesn't affect me at all. I shut the little door with a well-aimed kick. I switch on the TV and watch the news. In the open drawer of the night-stand I discover a little switch you can use while lying in bed to lock the door, turn out the light, and signal that you do not wish to be disturbed. After the news I leaf through the brochures scattered on the desk and glance at the offers for day trips to Caesarea and the Dead Sea. There's so much to do—maybe I'll stay here longer. I could easily carry on my business from this hotel, and I have enough saved up that I could live pretty comfortably for quite a while. By the time I go to sleep I'm astonished to realize that I haven't so much as glanced at the emergency exit plan, which is prominently displayed inside a glass case on the wall. The red lines affect me no more than the ice in the freezer.

WHEN I AWAKE the next day I'm alert to every sound, imagining that somehow Mrs. Kugelman will find me, that she will once again knock on my door. I've long since for-given her. How much I miss her round face. How beautiful the long mornings with her were: I should have savored every delicious minute.

A week goes by, and I can no longer bear it. Koby picks me up in his cab and takes me back to our old hotel. And there she is, waiting on the sofa in the lobby. But she no longer recognizes me. It hurts so much, I start to panic. I force myself to take a few deep breaths until I calm down, and then I stand in the corner of the lobby and watch her.

I see her eyes light up as she spots a boisterous young American, clearly the next person she wants to win over for Będzin. His cell phone is obnoxiously loud, but she doesn't seem to mind and sets off in pursuit as he heads upstairs. She moves more slowly than she did a week ago, and instead of her old umbrella she's using a proper cane. The stairs have become too difficult for her, but out of love for Będzin she has overcome her fear of elevators. She rides up to his floor. Soon she will knock on his door. Little does he suspect that soon his cell phone will be dead to the world for hours and hours.

WHEN I VISIT the hotel again a few days later, the sofa is empty. I spend the entire morning sitting in the lobby, reading the paper, waiting for her. I'm the first one who's ever asked about her, says the clerk. No one even noticed she wasn't there, although she's come every single day since he began working in the hotel. Startled by the news, I call Koby and ask him if I can book his services for the next few days. We circle the nearby streets searching for some sign of her, but all in vain. No one knows where she lives. We make the rounds of the large hotels along the beach, inquire with the police, in old-age homes, hospitals, social service stations. Not a trace. The old lady seems to have disappeared. If only I'd followed her once, in secret, then I'd know where she lives; if only I'd paid more attention, besieged her apartment at night, camped out in front with blankets and pillows, then she wouldn't have gotten away. Who will ever again tell me about my father's city? What is there left for me? I go back to my hotel and carefully open Halina's chest and lay out my eight forks and nine knives.

A WEEK LATER the khamsin has passed. I open the window of my room and inhale deeply. The sunlight seeps under my skin; the ice age is coming to an end. I close my eyes and taste the sea. In the dull gleam of the freshly washed windowpane I discover my reflection. Today I see myself as beautiful. My long hair flutters in the gentle draft, stroking my face. I like the way I look in my tight-fitting thin pants. I carefully brush my hair and reach for some red lipstick. I'll call Koby and tell him to pick me up and take me to his uncle's fish restaurant.

"And bring your brother, Eli," I tell him.

21

◄○►

My inheritance

THE HOT SUMMER GIVES WAY TO A MILD WINTER INTER-
spersed with warm, golden days. Here, the trees renew
themselves throughout the year; the withered leaves fall
almost imperceptibly to the ground while the bright buds
hurry to ripen in the green trees. A warming November
breeze flows through the wide-open window; the air is soft
as velvet. I have the feeling that I'm breathing pure sunlight.

I breathe, and the words begin to flow straight from the
Black Przemsza right onto the page. And young Bella Kugelman is coming back to life, cheerful and happy, as she was in
Będzin, running down Kołłątaj Street, waving to everyone
right and left. Her braids are swinging up and down, I reach
out and give a pull, and she laughs and says, "One chance is
all you get."

About the author

MINKA PRADELSKI, sociologist and documentary filmmaker, has spent decades exploring the psychological effects of the Holocaust on survivors—such as her own parents—and their children. An honorary member of Steven Spielberg's Shoah Foundation, she lives in Frankfurt, Germany. This is her first novel.

About the translator

PHILIP BOEHM'S most recent translation is *The Hunger Angel* by Herta Müller. Other translations from German and Polish include *Traces* by Ida Fink and *Words to Outlive Us: Eyewitness Accounts from the Warsaw Ghetto*. He has received awards from the National Endowment for the Arts, the UK Society of Authors, and the American Translators Association.